The Great Land Grab
by
Sam Hossler

D1527071

First published by:
Dog Ear Publishing
4010 W. 86th Street, Ste H
Indianapolis, IN 46268
www.dogearpublishing.net

ISBN: 978-159858-319-9
Library of Congress Control Number applied for

This book is printed on acid-free paper.
This book is a work of Fiction. Places, events, and situations in this book are purely Fictional and any resemblance to actual persons, living or dead, is coincidental.
Printed in the United States of America

Without the help of the following
I would never have been able to put this book together.
First my editor, Erin Wiedemer, who not only corrected
my grammar but furnished hints on how to make the
story flow, then, Leah Wiedemer, who painstakingly
designed and painted the cover and icons of Fort Pitt, and
last but certainly not least, Gerry Kuffer, without his help
and expertise the pages would never
have been formatted and correlated as you see them.

The Layout of Fort Pitt during the mid 1700s

Editor - Erin Wiedemer - web site - A Write Word
Cover & Design - Leah Wiedemer - web site l-wiedemer
Formatting - Gerry Kuffer

Index

Forward

In 1609, King James I granted a charter to the Virginia Colony giving them the land from sea to westward sea, though no one knew where the westward sea might lie. In 1681, King Charles II granted William Penn a charter, to repay a debt to Penn's father, which encompassed a large section of this same land. The squabbling between Pennsylvania and Virginia raged throughout the 1700s. Both Virginia and Pennsylvania were sending settlers to this westward frontier. Virginia granted 50 acres to each family that would homestead there; Pennsylvania sold the land to those willing to move west.

Fort Pitt was closed by order of King George in 1772, because, the British Crown reasoned, it had set a Royal Proclamation in 1763, which stated that the Indian lands west of the Ohio River were not to be invaded or granted to white settlers. In 1773, the Governor of Virginia, Lord Dunmore, sent Dr. John Connolly to the Three Rivers asserting his claim to the area for Virginia. Was it any wonder the two colonies both claimed this frontier? As Fort Pitt and Pittsburgh were the gateways to lands further into the interior, it was paramount to control them. The Proclamation of 1763 was virtually ignored.

Many politicians of the day held large tracks of land on this western frontier and were looking to cash in on their holdings. Lord Dunmore had holdings as far inland as what is now Louisville, Kentucky. George Washington, Patrick Henry, and others formed land companies and controlled large holdings in the western portion of Virginia, what is now West Virginia. The fact that their claims and claims of other land companies overlapped didn't seem to cause disputes.

During this land grabbing there was considerable unrest in the colonies. The Stamp Act of 1765, which placed large taxes on goods coming from England, was being bitterly contested. In Virginia the highhanded actions of Lord Dunmore was a constant irritation to the wealthy landowners. For these reasons, when shots were fired in April of 1775, a full-scale rebellion broke out.

Our story opens with the battle of Point Pleasant. Was this a contrived elimination of militia troops from both Virginia and Pennsylvania by Lord Dunmore? It has been called Dunmore's War. The accusations have never been proven, but history questions the motives behind this great land grab.

The Battle at Point Pleasant
Chapter 1

"Keep ya head down Murphy, ya goanna get us kilt," snarled Smitty to his companion as they stared at a sea of Indians through the morning mist.

"I just want to see how many they is," replied the Irishman.

The morning sun hadn't broken above the horizon, but streaks of reddish light were stabbing into the sky, giving just enough light to see forms moving through the light fog.

"They's more than you can count, ya stupid ole coot. The Colonel didn't send us out here to get kilt; we's to get information, and now we got it. Let's get the hell outta here."

"Too late! They's seen me; run for it," Murphy shouted. Both men jumped up from their prone positions and began running hunched over through

1

the waist high goldenrod. Musket balls whizzed past their bent forms as they zig-zagged across the open flat of high weeds.

"The trees is just ahead; if'n we can make that, we got a chance," Smitty spit his words out as if they held all of his distaste for the Irishman who had gotten them into this race against death. When he heard no reply he took a quick glance behind and saw Murphy convulsing among the goldenrod stocks. *Must a caught one in the back,* he thought without losing a step. Smitty increased his speed as much as he could. *I ain't as young as I was; the pain in my legs and chest caught me sooner than it used to. There, I made the trees, now to get to the camp.*

Somehow, by dodging through the thick forest, he eluded the arrows and bullets sent flying after him and came upon the outlying sentries who had been alerted when they heard the musket fire.

"They's a pack of 'em," Smitty called out between strangled breaths, as he raced past those guarding the far perimeter.

The four guards discharged their weapons and took flight with Smith for the outer barricade at the camp.

"Captain, Captain, they's a hundred of 'em after me. Get the troops," Smitty yelled as he came within shouting distance.

It was a needless warning as the officer had heard the gun fire and had a line of marksmen behind the fallen tree trunks and brush that lay along the little creek flowing into the Kanawha River. Unfortunately, he thought it was only a small party of Indians that could be easily repelled.

"I'm a telling ya, Sir, they's over a hundred. Murphy's been kilt, and we see'd more redskins than I ever saw," Smitty's words were broken and coming hard as his labored breathing choked the sounds. His lungs felt like they were going to explode, and his legs were unsure under his weight, as he bent over, trying to recover enough to get into the fight. "Cap', I'm a telling ya, we need more men."

The frontiersmen were pouring a deadly fire at the attacking, overwhelming foe. The sheer numbers of charging Indians made it obvious that they couldn't hold out for long. A runner had been sent back to the main force for reinforcements.

"Men, we need to hold out long enough for the troops to get here," the captain shouted above sounds of muskets being fired and men yelling to watch this side or that. In the morning fog, the white acrid smoke from the black powder being fired by both sides hung like a smothering blanket over the battlefield.

Fortunately, the runner met a troop of reinforcements, led by Colonel Lewis, the general's son, who had heard the gunfire and rallied his men, bringing them along at double time. Although it was a full regiment of frontiersmen in this relief party, they were still out numbered by three to one. Though the additional firepower enabled them to hold out for over an hour, they started to withdraw slowly back to the main camp where trees were cut and stacked as a makeshift fort. Just then another regiment showed up led by Colonel Fleming. Fleming called to the retreating men, bellowing encouragement and striding confidently up and down the firing line. With his fresh troops the battle line held.

"The Colonel's down," someone yelled as Colonel Lewis dropped to his knees. He had been hit by musket fire, and though he struggled to stay on his feet to give direction and moral, he finally collapsed, losing the battle between his will and the loss of blood. Colonel Fleming directed two men to carry the wounded commander back to the main camp.

4

Fleming ran along the battle line shouting to the men, "Watch the left side; pour your fire into the center; make each shot count," when suddenly a ball struck him down. Captain Gravley ordered him taken to the main camp and assumed command. Gravley hollered to the men carrying Fleming, "Tell the general we need more men; I don't know how long we can hold out."

Smitty was hunkered down beside a large maple tree, picking his shots as best he could. Suddenly, he felt a bump on his side and looked up, surprised to see his old friend Thompson slide beside him.

"Tommy, you ole son-of-a-gun, what the hell you doin' here?"

"I was in the neighborhood an' figured you could use some help," was the reply.

"Why, I ain't see'd you since we was a huntin' back in '70, or was it '72?"

Thompson spit out a stream of brown tobacco juice and smiled saying, "We can talk old times later; rit' now I think we got a problem."

The men were taking a beating, and the front line was starting to waver, struggling not to fall back. Some had already moved into position to retreat to the main camp. Their attackers saw this and grew wild with the anticipation of victory. Yelling and screaming insults at the defenders, the Indians rushed headlong into the battle line. Painted in red and black stripes they ran at full speed into the frontiersmen's fire.

"Smitty, it's gonna be hatchet and knife, get ready," Thompson yelled over the musket fire and screaming Indians.

"Looka thar, that be Colonel Field and his boys a comin' through the trees," Smitty replied happily.

The fresh troops brought new hope, and the men fought with renewed vigor. Tomahawks and long knives, pistols fired and then used as clubs, were now the weapons of choice in this close combat.

"Tommy, watch out," Smitty warned as an Indian leapt from the underbrush.

Thompson whirled, pulling the trigger of his long rifle as he turned. Puff went the powder in the frizen, before the explosion from the long barrel; the ball and flame caught the Indian full in the stomach. The half-inch chunk of lead stopped the foe's leap in mid air.

. "Ya' didn't kilt him, but you sure put a powerful lot of hurt to 'im," Smitty shouted.

Drawing his tomahawk, Tommy finished the uttering of the fallen warrior with a quick blow to the head.

Smitty had a long knife in one hand and a tomahawk in the other as he stepped out in front of a charging Indian. The surprised look on the painted face of the savage brought a smile to Smitty's as he rammed the long blade of English steel into his chest cavity and brought the tomahawk down with a crushing blow on the Indian's forehead.

"I'm gettin' too old for this," he muttered as he got ready to meet the next body rushing towards him.

Then, from behind his head, he heard the sputter and whoosh of a firing black powder rifle, and he saw the onrushing attacker lifted off his feet and thrown back to the ground. One of Field's men simply nodded as he calmly reloaded his weapon.

"I think they's fallin' back," Tommy shouted. "Sure enough, they's goin' back into the trees. Keep your head down; they's can still shoot."

The sun had passed overhead as the battle continued, with the Indians shooting sporadically from the trees, while the soldiers gathered their wounded and dead. General Lewis called three of his trusted captains,

"You think you could take your men and crawl along the lower edge of the bank of the Kanawha and up Crooked Creek to get behind those Injins?"

The main camp had the Kanawha River at its back, and a creek flowed into it on one side, with the Ohio River flanking the other. The frontiersmen had erected a barricade of tree trunks mortared with any debris they could pile up to give what little protection it could from an Indian onslaught. To a man they answered, "Yes."

As the afternoon sun moved across the sky, the Indians kept up a steady barrage of musket fire. Thompson and Smitty, secure behind their large maple tree trunk, would peek out just enough to locate a target, tell the other where it was, then poke out their heads just enough to make the Indian show himself when he tried to make a shot. This was the last mistake that Indian made.

The three companies of militia crept quietly and slowly along the water's edge; every man watching where he placed his feet, trying desperately to avoid the stones, tree roots and soft mud. They knew that any noise could reveal their position, and they wouldn't have a chance if they were trapped beneath the bank and the water. Once they were well beyond the Indian lines, up out of the creek bed they came, stealthily at first, until all were ready. Then with blood curdling shrieks they charged the rear of the Indian lines. Caught by complete surprise, the Indians broke and fell back to their camp beside the river.

Smitty asked Tommy,"You see the size of that one chief? He must be over six feet tall, and he had no fear; he walked around like bullets wouldn't dare touch him."

"Yep, that's Cornstalk, chief of the Shawnee. And did ya see that wild man with him? That's Logan; he's a chief of some sort, and does he ever hate the whites. I hear some white trash of John Connelly's got drunk and slit Logan's sister from stem to stern, and she was pregnant at the time. He's had it in for us ever since. I saw Cornstalk back at Fort Pitt last year when I was passin' through. You know they's closed the fort don't ya?"

The wounded were being carried back to the main camp, and the dead were gathered for a mass grave, while the Indians disposed of their dead by dropping them into the big river. Sentries were posted throughout the battle area, as no one was sure if another attack would descend upon them when the darkness of night closed in.

Walking back to the main camp, Smitty questioned Thompson, "Ya know Black Jack is with us? That puts the three of us plumb in the middle of things again. How'd ya decide to come a lookin' for a fight; and where ya been for two years?"

"Well, I came up outta the hills into what I thought was Fort Pitt, but found a bunch of no-goods runnin' the place. Then I heard about this here army bein' formed to clean out the Injins. So I thought it may be a good scrap, and I ain't been in one fur a spell. Besides, I heard if'n we fought, we could get 100 acres of land out here, and I'm ready to move," Tommy explained.

Smitty lifted one eyebrow and replied, "We just about only needed a small plot to get buried in, not 100 acres."

"Where's Black Jack and some of the other boys? Ya said they were with this outfit," Tommy questioned.

"This is the second time Dunmore held us up, makin' us short a meat. Since the general said we was to wait for Lord Dunmore and his army, about fifty a the scouts went out a huntin' this morning before light. Ya know we got almost 2,000 men to feed. I guess they was too far away to hear the ruckus or they'd a been back. Jack, like a bunch of 'em, lives south in the mountains that's bein' squabbled over by Virginia and Pennsylvania. Most a them don't care much for Dunmore, but the offer of free land brought 'em along," Smitty replied.

As the sun began sinking behind the western horizon, campfires were built and small groups of men gathered to heat water for tea and chew on what little jerky they had left.

"Well look at that," Thompson cried, "Jack's a carrying the scrawniest deer I've seen in years."

"Don't you make fun a my kill," Jack called back, "I chased this critter over half the mountainside just so you could have a taste a fresh venison. Where'd you come from anyway, ya ole troublemaker?"

Other hunters came into camp in small groups, some carrying deer and some with nothing. The animals were hung from tree limbs and skinned and butchered in short order. Jack cut the loins from his deer and brought them over to the fire along with another hunter he had paired up with.

"This here's Snipe; he's not a bad fellow for a flatlander." Jack said introducing his partner. "Snipe's from down around Williamsburg, and he's got some interesting news about this Lord Dunmore fellow." With that he began skewering the loins on long sticks, and when finished he placed them on the Y sticks on either side of the hot coals.

"While that's a heatin' maybe we can have a drop of the corn squeezin's I got squirreled away. I knowed I could use a hit, and from the looks a it, ya both could too," Tommy said with a faint smile. "I just happened to see ole Van Gilder when I was back a visitin' Griswalt, and he offered me a jug for ole times' sake. You'll see that his juice has improved over the last 10 years."

While the venison roasted, its fat dripped into the hot coals, causing little puffs of flame and smoke to shoot up. The jug was passed around, and Smitty went down to the creek and pulled up a bunch of cattail roots which he packed in mud and sat next to the fire.

"They's passable with a touch a salt," he explained as he reached for the jug.

"Snipe tells me this here Lord Dunmore has an army as big as ours and was supposed to meet up with us back yonder a ways," Jack stated as he took another pull on the jug. "But when we got there, a messenger shows up saying the general was to move on up here and he'll meet us. We been on the march for the better part of a month and our food is runnin' out. Now we get ambushed by the biggest war party we've ever run up against and still no Dunmore."

Snipe looked up in time to see a lieutenant he knew from Williamsburg walking by. "Hey Lieutenant," he called, "what's the word? Come on over, pull up a rock an have a snort."

Lieutenant Wadsworth smiled at the informal greeting from a lower rank militiaman and walked over and sat down. Ordinary citizens formed the frontier militia, and these men were mostly from the mountain regions. Self-reliant, but fearsome fighters, they had spent most of their adult lives fending for themselves without help or governing from a higher authority. Because of this, military etiquette was lax to non-existent. But they knew how to shoot and fight using the same tactics the Indians did: ambush and give no quarter. It was what kept them alive over the years.

"The lieutenant here knows all those high muckity-muck politicians back in Williamsburg. Maybe he can shed some light on why we's stuck here waitin' to get kilt," Snipe continued.

Wadsworth had a healthy pull on the jug and eyed the venison loin sizzling over the glowing coals.

"We's glad a the company, Lieutenant," Jack said. "You're welcome to share some a that meat with us."

Another pull on the jug and Wadsworth warmed up to the men who had fought so well and brought in the food the company so desperately needed. "Men," he announced, "we just got word that Lord Dunmore ain't meetin' us here. He sent word that we are to cross the big river and meet him at some Injin village, where he plans to make peace."

After another long swallow from the jug he continued, "This has riled everyone from the general on down. We don't know if'n those Injins are a waiting up river for us to come or not, but I guess we'll find out tomorrow morning.

"Ya know there's a couple a land companies layin' claim to this surrounding territory? Dunmore owns one of 'em, and the big politicians like Washington, Patrick Henry, and others have claims as well. They's had surveyors out as far as the furthest Injin territory, layin' out tracks a land. Makes no difference that in 1763, the Crown said there would be no more expansion into Indian lands. Nobody paid any attention to that then, and they sure ain't now.

"What really galls my hide is that Dunmore is tryin' to renege on his promise of 100 acres for each man here. He figures to get that land for his self. Do you think it was a coincidence that we got left out here to fight this enormous war party by ourselves? D'you know they was Delawares, Mingos, Iroquois, Wyandotts, and Shawnees in that bunch that tried to way-lay us?

"Back in Williamsburg, Patrick Henry is a colonel in the militia, and he wouldn't bring his troops on this mission. That tells us something. Besides, Dunmore has been tryin' to break the militia 'cause he's afraid of 'em. There's talk he might even try ta confiscate all of the militia's gunpowder. Now, that would cause a sure enough ruckus. So there's a lot goin' on that makes this trip into Injin territory more than just cleanin' out the savages who been raidin' the settlers."

Thompson, who had been listening intently, spoke up asking, "Who's this John Connolly that's taken over Fort Pitt and runnin' roughshod over the people? He even changed the name a the fort to Fort Dunmore."

"Ah, that's another story about our Governor Dunmore." Wadsworth said. "But it will hold while we chew on some of that great smellin' venison."

Fresh meat, corn liquor, and fatigue cut the story telling short as the men rolled into their blankets, exhausted and stomachs full to fall asleep.

Chapter 2
The Peace Treaty

Long before fingers of light reached into the Eastern sky, trees were being cut, and a rough barricade set up, to give what little protection it could to the wounded that must be left behind.

"Jack, ya shoulda seen them Injins," Smitty called to his friend as they prepared to break camp. "That big 'en, Cornstalk, would stride back and forth, yelling something to his braves, and when one tried to turn and run that ole son-a-gun split his head wide open with his tomahawk. You can bet that kept the rest of 'em in line."

"Yep, we've seen two or maybe three different tribes fight together, but this was a whole band a Injins I never saw before," Tommy added.

Lieutenant Wadsworth and Snipe came by just then.   "Men, we got orders to move. The scouts claim the Injins are gone; they must have slipped across the river during the night. Orders from Dunmore are sending us to meet him at some place in the Ohio Territory. I'll tell you, the general is in a rage. His son died yesterday along with a bunch a mighty fine men and he's thirsty for revenge."

"Jack, how about you, Thompson, and Smitty go scoutin' out ahead; I don't favor walkin' into an ambush," Lieutenant Wadsworth suggested.

This suited the three old rangers just fine. It was the type of work they did best, and it kept them out of the military main stream.

Upon arriving at the Indian encampment, it was obvious that this was where Cornstalk and Logan had taken their army across into territory that, by treaty, had been designated for the Indians alone. What wasn't generally known was that Daniel Boone had made an expedition three years earlier into the Kentucky territory to make a treaty and purchase land from the Cherokees. In fact, a surveying party was there now, laying out tracks for land speculation.

Just the year before, almost to the day, a party of Boone's was attacked in Powell's Valley by a band of Shawnee. Boone's sons were among those killed and this ended, for the time being, his attempt to settle in the Kentucky wilderness.

"Jack, there's a canoe still pulled up on shore. Mind how ya show yourself; they might still be some around," Smitty whispered.

From out of the bushes came the call, "Hello Rangers."

The three woods-wise frontiersmen had spread out as they approached the now empty campsite and looked one to another in wonder at being caught flatfooted by an unknown voice that seemed to know them. Then an image appeared out of the shadowy light and morning mist, clad in buckskin and carrying a long rifle.

"Ya don't remember yer old playmate from Griswalt's?" he asked.

"Ya sound like that young squirt Jacob, from the Mock farm," Jack called back. "Only ya aged a little and got a face full a whiskers."

"Well, I'll be damned," stammered Thompson. "What a ya doin' out here in the middle a nowhere?"

Not waiting for a reply, the three rushed forward to shake hands with Jacob and learn how and why he was hiding in the bushes of the Indian campsite.

"It appears your friends left here in the middle of the night," Jacob said.

"They ain't no friends and they's as mean as rattlesnakes," Smitty muttered between spits of tobacco juice. "You been a couple hours earlier and your hair might be decoratin' some lodge pole."

"Fortunately, I camped about five miles up river last night, so I never saw a hair of 'em," the newcomer explained.

"We're heading across to scout out the territory and find where these rascals might be. The rest of the army is just over that rise, so we best get started, and since you were kind enough to bring us a boat we won't even get wet. Want to come along?" Jack waved his arm toward the far shore as he spoke.

Jacob never answered, just walked to the canoe and climbed in. As they paddled for the far shore, Jacob explained how he happened to end up on the banks of the Ohio in hostile country.

"I was visiting my folks back in Westmoreland County when word came about this army headin' into Indian Territory to settle the savages down. Well, I guess you didn't know I went out to the Ohio Territory and homesteaded a chunk a land in the area where we were back in '64. Remember how I liked that land? Anyway, the land company has some surveyors out in Kentucky, and they figure if there's gonna be fightin' they best tell these fellows to get out or lie low. So, me an a couple others took the job a findin' them and lettin' 'em in on the war. I liberated this here canoe and figured to travel down river to Kentucky. The others went over land, which seemed like a long walk to me. So here I am. I saw this campsite and decided to check it out when I heard you all comin' through the brush.

"Ya know that a guy,Connolly, has taken over the fort and the town? He's a mean snake, stirrin' up the Injins. Why he had his men shoot down a whole party of Shawnee chiefs when they came to pow-wow in the town. Kilt the whole bunch, they did. Word is, he's got a big interest in cleanin' the Injins outta here so's he and his cronies can take over the land. The more he gets the Injins riled up and a fightin' with us farmers, the more excuse he has to wipe them out."

Thompson scowled, "Lieutenant Wadsworth started to tell us about him last night but never finished. Seems the lieutenant knows a lot about the politicians down Williamsburg way. The way him and the other

21

officers was a actin' this morning, I'll bet they's more to this than just settling these redskins down."

"Why do ya suppose Dunmore keeps changin' where we's to meet him? I think Snipe might have a point when he says that the governor just may be a lookin' to get rid of a lot a fightin' men, who don't take kindly to him takin' their land and causin' him grief over his high handed ways. And, boy, don't go callin' me captain; I ain't a captain no more and these fellows got their own captains. I'm just a scout like Smitty and Tommy here," Jack declared as they stepped on the shore of the Ohio Territory.

"Looka here," called Smitty pointing to moccasin tracks in the soft shoreline soil. "About half the bunch went off inland, but the others headed up river into that thick brush."

"They may be settin' up an ambush," Jack muttered, "or they might just be a watchin' to see how strong our army is. Either way I don't like it. Tommy, why don't you go back and let the lieutenant know so's they can be ready if anything happens. We'll check out the trail inland and cut back to see if we can find where them other no-goods went."

Thompson was in the canoe and shoving off before Jack finished his statement. *Sure glad we have this here canoe,* he thought to himself as he paddled back to the other side. The advance party of the army was just coming to the Indian camp site when he pulled up on shore. Lieutenant Wadsworth was leading the group and held up his hand when he saw Tommy coming toward him.

"We tracked 'em to the other side where they split up," Tommy informed the lieutenant without preamble. "About half of them headed into the bush and the rest headed inland. Split up like that, I don't think they's plannin' to attack, but I don't know they ain't either."

Wadsworth called to his men, "Start building those rafts; we've got to get the army across as soon as possible." Then to Thompson he explained, "The general had us build a rough barricade for the wounded and a company of men will stay behind to protect them while the rest of us go on to meet Dunmore out by a place called Camp Charlotte."

Thompson noted the lieutenant never referred to the governor as Lord Dunmore or even Governor Dunmore, only by his last name. It was a clear indication that he had little respect for the man.

Meanwhile, Smitty, Jack, and Jacob were spread out, following the obvious trail left by the retreating Indians. Jacob had elected to go into the bush looking for signs of the split off party, while Jack and Smitty kept on the tracks of the main group.

Jacob came back with the news, "They's dogin' us!" he exclaimed. "I couldn't tell if they had ideas of attackin', but they're watchin' every move we make, and some are back at the river waitin' for the army to come across. If they was goin' kill us, they'd a done it by now. I figure they just want to keep us in sight, and maybe if they get real brave they'll attack the army once it starts across the water."

"If'n they'd planned that they wouldn't have split up," Jack speculated. "My guess is they are just to keep doggin' us and the army until Cornstalk decides what to do."

The three scouts reached a rolling open area that Jacob told them was called Pickway Plains.

"How come you know so much about this territory?" Jack questioned Jacob.

Jacob half smiled and decided to tell his companions his story. "Well, I told you I was farmin' the area where we went in '64; what I didn't tell you was after I started building my cabin, the local Indians came a callin'. Not that they were upset with me, they just wanted to see why I was buildin' a house. Every one else that had come through never stayed. The chief was a nice old guy that had a good lookin' daughter. At least I thought she was good lookin', but I'd been away for quite a spell. To make a long story short, I bought her. They call it married, but we just kind a live together. She taught me the lingo and we would take trips around the territory visitin' other tribes an' her relatives. So I learned their ways and the lay a the land.

"This Injin, Logan, came through, riling up the tribes, gettin' them to join together for this here army to keep the whites outta their land. Our chief, my father-in-law, suggested I go back and visit my folks until this whole thing blows over. So I did. Then they was lookin' for men to let the surveyors know to get outta Kentucky and here I am.

"From what I could find out, this Chief Cornstalk was against a war, but Logan and the other hot heads pushed for it, so Cornstalk took up the tomahawk and led this mixture of tribes in an all out war. I had no idea they were camped on the river a waitin' for you, or I would a got here earlier and let ya know."

As the trio sat under a large tree, a figure clad in buckskin emerged from the far side of the field. "Who do ya suppose that be?" Smitty queried.

Obviously the stranger had seen them and was headed in their direction. When he came within hailing distance, he shouted that he was looking for General Lewis.

"Come set a spell," Jack returned, "he'll be along directly. Ya seen any Injins on your way?"

The new comer sat down with them and explained he was a messenger from Lord Dunmore and had new orders for General Lewis.

"Where the hell is this here Lord Dunmore and his army?" Smitty asked. "Ya know we was damn near wiped out back at the river where we was supposed to meet him two days ago. The men ain't real happy. We been followin' two separate bunches a them Injins, ya sure ya didn't see any?"

"I seen 'em a watching you and me on my way in," was the reply. "The main camp of 'em is at Camp Charlotte, but from what I hear they's a bunch doggin' the general and his army, that's why they sent me with new orders."

Jack wasn't sure about this scout or "messenger," as he preferred to be called. "Well, ya might as well rest your bones; they'll be here about sundown. We weren't in any hurry so they could catch up. But I don't like the idea a having a band a savages followin' us and them."

"I'm Wilson," the newcomer said, "Lord Dunmore is meetin' with Cornstalk and some others to make a treaty."

"Why? So's they can ambush us again?" Smitty snorted.

"I don't know nothin', but that I'm to deliver this paper to the general. So if'n ya don't mind, I'll just wait here with y'all 'till he gets here."

It didn't much matter if the three minded or not, Wilson was staying, and they didn't really have a say about it. The sun was low in the western sky when Lieutenant Wadsworth and his troop arrived. "The rest are right behind us," he told the four waiting.

By dark the army had gathered and General Lewis had called for his officers. Wilson was brought to Wadsworth to deliver the message.

"What the hell does he mean?" the general could be heard bellowing across the whole camp.

Wilson turned pale when he saw the rage on the general's face. He considered running, but a bevy of colonels, majors, captains, and lieutenants had blocked any retreat he might have had.

General Lewis read the orders to the assembled officers. "We are ordered to stop, as we may jeopardize the peace treaty Lord Dunmore is arranging with the Indians. Have the men ready to move out at sun up. We're going to see about this peace treaty. I've lost my son and over a hundred other good Virginians, and we got a war party a doggin' us from the rear. No sir, we're going on."

Wilson couldn't wait to get out of there and on his way back to Dunmore. He knew it wasn't safe to travel at night, but it sure wasn't safe to be at the general's camp after delivering that message either.

The army of General Lewis was on the move before the sun had cracked above the skyline. The men were outraged that they had been treated so poorly. With rumors flying through the ranks that Dunmore had set them up to be massacred, these backwoodsmen had only revenge on their minds.

The collective rage moved the army at unbelievable speed, and by mid afternoon another messenger arrived to stress that Lord Dunmore had ordered the army back to Point Pleasant. When some of the troops drew their tomahawks and started toward him, that bearer of ill tidings departed with all the haste he could muster. By late afternoon the troops were within three miles of Camp Charlotte. Here the general ordered camp to be set, and men he could trust were put on special sentry duty--not to guard the camp, but to keep his mutinous men from invading the governor's camp and killing Dunmore.

Dunmore was terrified of these wild frontiersmen. He had heard how they had defeated the larger Indian force at Point Pleasant and that his plans to cheat them out of the land promised was now common knowledge.

With a contingent of his most trusted men, Dunmore and an Indian Chief named White-Eyes came to Lewis' camp. White Eyes was a representative of Chief Cornstalk and it was a near fatal mistake to bring him to the camp as it was all the sentries could do to keep the frontiersmen from scalping the governor and killing White Eyes. Calm was finally restored without any bloodshed. Lord Dunmore told Lewis that a peace treaty had been reached and Lewis had to take his men back to Point Pleasant, pick up the wounded and others, and return to where they had started from, then disband the army.

That evening Lieutenant Wadsworth and Snipe came by the campfire of Jack, Smitty, Thompson, and Jacob. "Men," he said, "we been played a bad hand. But, Dunmore won't be gettin' all this land he's been hankerin' for either. Before I left Williamsburg, I heard that Lord Dartmouth, who's the Secretary of State for the Colonies, issued an order from the Privy Council in Whitehall that all this land and then some was to be granted to a colony called Vandalia. Some of the owners of this outfit are Benjamin Franklin, Thomas Walpole and Samuel Wharton.

"We know George Washington, Patrick Henry, and some others are in this land deal with Dunmore, so now that the high muckity-mucks have given it to another company, the fur should fly. And there's no love lost between these Virginia leaders, even if they are in bed with each other. They're all out to make money and don't care how they get it. Dunmore is on shaky ground with the Crown and the Virginia planters. So I guess this whole thing was for not, at least for now.

"Snipe and I are headin' back to Williamsburg. I sense trouble brewin' there."

Jacob looked at the others and said, "I guess I'll go back to my farm and woman. She's ready to give birth anytime now. Hopefully the trouble has died down enough to live a normal life."

Jack looked at his two friends, "What say we go back down to the hills and do a little huntin', trappin', and lots a drinkin'? I do want to stop by Fort Pitt an see what's goin' on."

"I'm fer the drinkin' part, so I guess I'll do the rest just to keep ya happy," Smitty chimed in. "What say, Tommy? Want to rest your bones with a jug?"

Tommy's eyes lit up, "You bet. We're gettin' too old for this here fightin' anyway. I think we ought a stop by Van Gilder's and pick up a couple jugs."

"What ya mean a couple?" Jack sneered. "We'd better get a barrel to last the winter."

That brought smiles all around.

Jack told Jacob, "We'll look in on your folks and tell 'em you be fine."

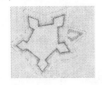

Chapter 3

Westmoreland County January 1774

"Well, Amos how was your New Year's eve?" Griswalt asked as he poured a tankard of homebrew for Amos Mock.

Mock looked up, smiled, and said, "Just about as much excitement as any other year. Sam and Jenny came down for dinner, Roy was off huntin' up river, an Dorothy and Rebecca are still in Philadelphia."

"How's Sam and his new bride doin'? They got that cabin finished just in time before winter set in. That old Comstock place is a nice piece a ground. The boys kept the crops growin' all these years so Jenny had a decent dowry from sellin' corn an barley to Van Gilder," the innkeeper responded.

"Yep, that money bought 'em tools and such to set up house keepin'. Sam's a worker; he not only worked their fields, an built the cabin, but helped me, Jonahs, an Roy cut hay and gather the crops. He'll make a good farmer an' that ground will support about anything he wants to grow. Did ya taste any a the liquor Van Gilder made from the barley he grew? It'll bring a premium for sure."

Then, changing the subject, Mock asked, "What's the word on the fort. Since it's been closed we got little to no protection. The Rangers been disbanded, and there's no militia to speak of. I know the Injins are supposed to be peaceable, but it won't take much to set off that hothead Logan. His family, at least his sister and husband, are nice enough. I've seen 'em once or twice when I went to town. But, that half breed Logan is a boilin' pot waitin' to spill over."

"A fellow was in just the other day sayin' he heard the Governor of Virginia, Lord Dunmore, was sendin' a bunch to take over the fort and declare we are under his rule. From what he said the leader of these men is a John Connolly who's in cahoots with Dunmore on a big land grab," Griswald answered.

"I wonder what Judge Crawford will have to say?" Mock questioned. "They're supposed to be holdin' court this month over at Hanna's Town. If push comes to shove, we ain't got a militia to protect us from these outlaws. I got my land from Pennsylvania an so did you; what's gonna happen if this Virginia bunch takes over?"

Griswald shook his head, "I wish Captain Jack and his Rangers were still around; I'd feel a lot safer. When they pulled the army out, they left us damn near defenseless. Them sittin' in Philadelphia and London got no idea what's goin' on out here. But I guess it's better than it was 10 years ago."

Mock smiled at that comment. "Yep I guess you're right on that. When them Injins hit your place in '63, I thought we was goners fer sure. If it hadn't been for Jack and the others, we woulda' been too."

"I hear he's still livin' down in the mountains. That's plumb in the heart of the country Virginia claims is theirs. I wonder whose side he'd be on if'n it comes down to a fight? He wasn't any to pleased when the Crown set the import tax on us, but I don't know how he sets with Virginia," Griswalt replied.

As the two men picked up their mugs for another swallow, the door burst open.

"They's here, them no-accounts from Virginia," Walt Grimes, the mail rider, shouted as he erupted into the tavern, out of breath and red faced from over extending his physical capabilities. "I was in town pickin' up the mail for the East, and this bunch rode in wavin' their long guns and war clubs. Them claimin' they was Virginia militia an were takin' over the fort and settin' up Virginia law. Un that's not all, he's changin' the name of the fort to Fort Dunmore, and he's now the Captain Commandant of the Militia. His word is law, he said, and his men would be there to back him up."

Griswalt couldn't believe what he was hearing and stood dumfounded, staring in disbelief at the man bringing such news. Amos Mock was equally shocked, but simply said he best get home and alert his family to the pending trouble.

Grimes downed a quick tankard of grog and headed out the door shouting, "I'm stopping at Magistrate St. Clair's place. He'd better know the happenin's before this gets outta hand."

"Outta hand," Griswalt stammered, "it's already outta hand and we got nothin' but a couple a constables to protect us.

* * * *

Fortunately, the magistrates were already meeting at Hanna's arrived, again out of breath and red faced, to relay his story to the court. The magistrates were loyal Pennsylvania subjects, and this invasion of their territory was serious indeed. Over the next few days, warrants for the arrest of John Connolly were drawn up, and the local constables gathered for serving them. No one thought it would be easy, so as many men as they could get to volunteer were pressed into service to present a show of strength.

Grimes was sent back to Pittsburgh to keep an eye on the actions and where-abouts of the Virginia group. Grimes returned to Hannah's Town within two days of his departure. "Judge," he shouted upon entering, "ya won't believe what happened when I got back to Pittsburgh. Ya remember the party a Shawnee chiefs that was meetin' in town? Well, Connolly an his bunch ambushed 'em an killed the whole lot of 'em. I mean all a 'em, and with no reason."

Arthur St. Clair had drafted a letter to Governor Penn advising him of the invasion of Pennsylvania, and he now added the atrocities to the complaint. "We've got to act now," St. Clair told his colleagues. "This behavior can not be tolerated. Assemble the constables and have the warrant served. Bring this Connolly here, and we'll jail him until a trial can be set."

The constables, and as many armed friends as they could assemble, marched into Pittsburgh, ready for the fight everyone anticipated. However, what they found was a drunken bunch of Virginia militia. Some, that could still stand were chasing the few women they could find, the others had passed out where they had fallen after a night of drinking. It didn't take long to find Connolly, arrest him, and head back to Hanna's Town.

"I'm the Captain Commandant," Connolly shouted as they led him away. "You have no jurisdiction over me or my men. This is Virginia territory. I'll see you shot for this!"

Assembled at the courthouse were St. Clair, Ennis Mackay, Devereux Smith, and Andrew McFarlane, all justices of the Pennsylvania Court. Sentencing was swift, but a bail was established. Connolly paid it and fled the territory. It didn't take long for the news to travel throughout the countryside, and it was a frequent topic of conversation at Griswalt's.

"I'll bet that Connolly was taken down a peg or two," Griswalt would tell all who stopped by for a pint. "We'll show that Governor Dunmore who's a runnin' this territory."

Then Roy Mock brought news that all of Connolly's men hadn't left with him. "That renegade from Connolly's bunch got drunk and picked a fight with the Indian Logan family. Killed Logan's sister's husband, and when she came runnin' to his aid, that no-good slit her open stem to stern, and she was pregnant at the time. Logan has no use for us anyway, now he'll go on a rampage for sure. Too bad he wasn't home with them at the time; he would have settled that argument in a hurry."

"I heard Logan has been a raiding up and down the river with his band," Griswalt added. "When he gets word of this, there'll be hell to pay. Better keep a sharp eye out for any unusual action."

* * * *

Dr. John Connolly wasn't one to give up power and potential wealth easily. As soon as he was released from the Hanna's Town jail, he headed straight for Augusta County, Virginia. The Virginia government considered everything north and west of Staunton, Virginia, the County seat of Augusta County, to be Virginia territory. This included the majority of Westmoreland County and Pittsburgh. The sheriff of Augusta County was only too happy to swear Connolly in as a Justice of the Peace of Augusta County. Now Connolly felt he not only had the governors blessing to take over Pittsburgh and the fort, but the legal authority to do so as well. Connolly gathered 150 armed men as his constables, and in April of 1774, he returned to Pittsburgh. Court was in session at Hanna's Town when the contingent of Connolly's men and Connolly himself barreled into the courtroom.

"There will be no court held here," he declared as he set armed men at the door to keep the jurists from conducting business.

President Judge of Westmoreland County, William Crawford, strongly objected, as did St. Clair, Mackay, Smith, and McFarlane, who all had cases pending. After negotiations, Connolly agreed that the court might hear small cases of local interest, but he would have jurisdiction over all, and if he felt it was a matter of importance, he alone would hear the case. For three days the business of the court was conducted while armed men watched and threatened those involved. Mackay, Smith, and McFarlane lived in Pittsburgh, and when court ended, they returned home. Though not for long, as Connolly had his men storm their homes and arrest them. They were then sent off to jail in Staunton, Virginia.

Griswalt's became a beehive of activity. Men from as far away as Kittanning gathered to try and decide what could be done.

"Men," shouted Roy Mock, taking charge. "We aren't strong enough to fight this rabble that's taken over the fort and town, and for now they ain't bothered us outlying folks. At least not yet! Letters have been sent to Governor Penn and the Privy Counsel by our judges. We stood off the Injins and we can stand off these Virginians. I hear talk that we should just pull up stakes and move up to Kittanning. I for one ain't leavin'."

That brought a loud grumble of approval. Sam Mock, who had been sitting in the corner observing the hostile environment finally called to his brother, "I just saw Grimes, and he had some news. Judge Mackay was released from the Staunton jail to go and talk with Lord Dunmore. If'n you know Mackay, he can talk a wolf outta his dinner. In the mean time, Lord Dartmouth and Governor Penn are puttin' the pressure on Dunmore to stop this fightin' over who owns our territory."

Van Gilder spoke next, "Men, I just got back from makin' a delivery to Pittsburgh, and those folks are terrified. This Connolly is runnin' roughshod over everything and everyone. The fellow that's been floating the ferry back and forth across the river for years has had it taken off him, and one of Connolly's bunch took it over. I think it's just a matter of time before them scoundrels decide to come out here."

Chapter 4

Trouble Moves To The Hills

"Jenny, I'm going to the south field to pull stumps. Roy's bringing the oxen up; we'll be back about noon time," Sam Mock called to his new bride who was hanging out some washed clothes on a line in front of the cabin. The big iron pot sat over the almost spent fire, steam rising from the boiled water. Lye soap and dirty clothes had turned the water a murky gray, and it would need to be dumped when Sam and Roy came in for their noon meal.

Jenny called back waving her arm, "I'll have dinner ready for you," and went back to her chore. Muttering to herself, *I wish he'd get a well dug, this haulin' water up from the creek is gettin' old.*

The young couple were still getting their new home in shape. This past winter had been their first together, and although they had all the comforts most couples had, it took some getting used to--being alone, away from their families for the first time. Though they had grown up together as if they were brother and sister, (the Mocks took Jenny in after an Indian raid murdered her entire family and burnt their cabin to the ground) love blossomed between them in their teenage years. Now in their twenties, they married and settled on the old farm land that Jenny had inherited.

Sam had just left sight when Jenny looked up from her chore to see two riders turning from the trail and heading toward the cabin. *Should I ring the bell?* She wondered. *But no, that's silly. Why would anyone bother me out here?*

Sam had hung a large cast iron bell in the tree beside the cabin in case Jenny wanted him when he was in the field. They had never needed it, and Jenny only rang it when dinner or supper was ready and Sam hadn't come in from working the fields. She began to worry that she should ring it now, but it was already too late; the riders were less than a 100 yards away.

I don't like the looks of these two, Jenny thought. *They look downright mean.*

"Hello there little missy," the one with a large scar across his face called. "Your man about? We got business to talk."

"He's coming right back," Jenny lied. "What do you want?"

The other one with a big, unruly black beard spit a stream of tobacco juice into Jenny's vegetable patch, which had just been tilled for planting. Then he reined his horse into the soft dirt and sent another stream of the brown liquid into the ground.

"I'll go call him," Jenny said making a move to the side of the cabin.

It was a move too late, however, as the first rider spurred his horse between her and the cabin.

"Now don't you fret, little missy. We be the tax collectors. Yes sir, we been sent by the Commandant himself to collect your taxes." With that both men dismounted and started towards her. Before Jenny could run, they had her by the arms.

The black bearded one questioned, "You got any gold or silver coins to pay us with?" Then he spat again.

Jenny stammered, "We don't have any money; the crops ain't even planted yet."

The men could see the terror in this young woman's eyes. It brought hungry smiles to their faces, revealing sets of snaggled, yellowish green, tobacco stained teeth. The man's carnivorous maw emerging through the grizzled and matted black beard made him look all the more wild and menacing. "Claude, maybe if'n she got no money we could take payment out in trade?" the pock marked intruder suggested. This made black beard's grin even broader.

Jenny tried to scream, but the first rider clamped his dirty hand over her mouth as they dragged her inside the cabin.

It was just past noon when Sam and his brother, Roy, came up to the cabin. "There's no smoke comin' from the chimney," Roy observed.

"I don't like the looks a this," Sam replied as he rushed in through the cabin's door. "Jenny, you all right?" he shouted, before he saw her crouched in the corner. "Jenny, honey, what's the matter?"

Sobbing uncontrollably, Jenny tried to explain what had happened. The terror of the Indian raid years before flooded back into her memory; the attack and rape on the same land drove her into seclusion within her own mind.

"Gather her up; we'll take her down to Mother. And bring your rifle, we got some trackin' to do," Roy told his brother. Sam didn't reply but gathered his rifle and possible bag, made sure it had a supply of lead balls and priming powder, picked up Jenny, and headed out the door.

Margaret Mock took charge of Jenny as she had done after the Indian raid. Amos, the boys' father, came in from the field and heard the story the two brothers had pieced together.

"We got four, maybe five, hours a daylight; let's get goin'," Amos said to the boys who were anxious to get on with the business of tracking down the two tax collectors.

Roy tucked his tomahawk in his belt, "I ain't used this in ten years, but it will come in handy today."

Amos gave Sam a skinning knife, and stuck another one in his own belt. "These may come in handy too," he stated.

Back at the trail, the tracks weren't hard to follow. The hoof prints in the garden plot showed that one horse had a broken shoe, so tracking wouldn't be a problem.

"They's headin' straight for Griswalt's," Roy mumbled as he studied the broken horseshoe print.

"Let's cut down through the gully and over the hill. Bein' on foot, we can make up some time. And if'n they're drinkin' at Griswalt's, we can kill 'em there," Sam said, without a change of expression.

"Whoa, boy, we can't just kill 'em without a trial," Amos called back.

Roy shot a look of determination at his father and said, "The hell you say? I'm for doin' the work we need to do."

"Let's see what we find before we go makin' plans," Amos replied.

"Watch these sticker bushes," Roy called as he pushed his way down the steep hillside. "I don't remember them bein' this bad when we were youngins, but they's a lot I don't remember anymore."

"Things is just startin' to green up. When these bushes get growin' you won't be chargin' through here," Sam replied.

"Hold up," Amos snapped as they topped the rise outside of the tavern. "Two horses are tied up to the front of Griswalt's. Sam, you go around back in case they make a break for the window. Roy, you an' me will just walk in and see what's what before we do anything."

47

Pushing the door open, the two men stepped into the darkened room. Claude and his partner sat at a wooden table, jug in hand, passing it back and forth.

"Amos, these are John Connolly's tax collectors," Griswalt said with a scowl on his face. "Claims we owe back taxes all up and down the valley and hills."

Claude looked up at the two new comers and spit out, "You gotta pay, or we'll slap ya in jail."

Roy responded by thumbing the hammer back on his long rifle. The bloodshot eyes of the tax collectors widened. "Ya just been over to my brother's place, un visited with his wife, didn't ya?" Roy snarled.

Amos had moved to the side to better cover the criminals. "We come ta pay ya what we owe ya."

Claude shot up from his chair and made a run for the door. Just as he swung it open, Roy's hand, in a blur of motion, had his tomahawk from his belt and sent it straight into the spine of the tax collector. "Damn, I must be gettin' rusty; I was aimin' for his head," Roy said, as he turned to the remaining agent of John Connolly.

Sam came around to the door and reached down to pull the blade from the quivering body. "Should I finish 'im off?" he asked calmly.

"After bit," Amos replied, and turned to face a now terrified assailant. "You know what you did at that cabin is gonna cost you your life. Now, who are ya, and what are ya doin' in these parts?"

Gristwalt, his voice quaking with emotion, choked out, "Amos, these men were sent by Connolly. There'll be hell to pay. Take 'em to Hanna's Town and have 'em locked up."

"With Connolly runnin' things, what chance do ya think we'd have of gettin' justice?" Roy countered, as he grabbed a length of rawhide and began binding the man's hands behind his back.

Amos explained to Griswalt how the two men had ravished Jenny. "We'll deal out the justice here," he confirmed.

"I'm an honest tax collector," the prisoner whined. "It was all Claude's idea; I never had anything to do with it."

Sam bent down beside him, rage boiling, eyes blazing, skinning knife gripped tightly in a trembling hand. Suddenly, in a swift motion, he sliced off the man's ear. With cold calculation, he picked up the cartilaginous flesh and stuffed it in the screaming mouth of the terrified tax collector.

"That'll keep him quiet," Sam said as he straightened up.

"Well, what ya gonna do with 'em ?" Griswalt asked. "Ya can't take 'em to court and ya can't leave 'em here. An' this fellow seems to be chokin' on his ear."

"What d'ya think a that, Sam? He cut off his own ear and tried to eat it; now he's a chokin'." Roy looked at his brother with a slight smile.

"By golly, you're right. His eyes are a rollin' back in his head an' he's turnin' a funny color," Sam observed.

"Gimme my hatchet; I'll finish 'em," Roy decided nonchalantly.

"Not in here," Griswalt shouted. "There's enough blood around; I'll have a time cleanin' it up."

Grabbing the choking victim by the hair, Roy drug him to the door, over the still quivering body of his friend, and out by the horses. Before anyone else could get outside it was over.

"Help me load these two on their horses. I'll take 'em up over the ridge and turn 'em loose. If they's ever found it'll be the work a some renegade Injins," Roy stated.

"Just get 'em outta here," Griswalt pleaded.

"See y'all back home," Roy called as he led the horses with their cadaverous loads off down the trail, little puffs of dust rising as the hoofs struck the dry earth.

Griswalt was already pouring buckets of water on the blood stained floor; scrubbing on his knees with a sturdy brush and lye soap, erasing any evidence that might attract attention.

Margaret Mock had gotten Jenny cleaned up and into bed by the time the men returned home. "I got her to take a cup of herb tea; that seemed to calm her a bit. She's still scared and cryin' in her sleep, but I think she'll be right in a few days. How'd you boys make out?" Margaret asked worriedly.

"Things is taken care of," Amos replied. "Roy will be back about dark, so keep somethin' hot for his supper. Sam how about you goin' and gatherin' up the oxen? I don't want them wandering around with strangers about."

Silently, Sam picked up his rifle and headed back to his farm. The sun had sunk behind the hills when he returned, leading the two massive creatures. Neither his mother nor father said anything about the tear stains that streaked the dust on his face.

"How is she?" he asked as he propped his rifle beside the door.

"She's sleeping," his mother replied. "She's a strong girl; she'll make it."

* * * * *

Magistrate Arthur St. Clair was huddled at a table in Griswalt's with two other magistrates, Mackay and Smith. "Men, we can't hold court at Hanna's Town. Only Judge Crawford seems to have that privilege. And things are getting out of hand with Connolly running roughshod over the territory. I got a letter here, ready to send to Governor Penn, and I would like your signatures on it," St. Clair said in hushed tones.

Mackay picked up the conversation, "When I was at Williamsburg to see Dunmore, a delegation from Penn came down, but I don't think it did them any good. Dunmore is an arrogant sod. Even though Lord Dartmouth has complained to him about his actions, he openly defies him. Also, while I was there, I talked with some of the local politicians. Apparently, things aren't going real smooth for Dunmore at home. Word is, he's trying to raise an army to clean out the Indians in the Ohio and Kentucky territory. The Royal Proclamation of 1763 means nothing to him. He don't care if the Crown tells settlers to stay this side of the river or not. I heard that Dunmore and some others have formed a land company and are claiming everything West, wherever it goes."

"We got problems right here," St. Clair broke in. "Judge Crawford is leaning more and more to the Virginia side of the territory claim. What was it; three, four, weeks ago them tax collectors disappeared? Crawford gave the order to send Connolly's constables to find out what happened. We know they was here drinkin' and left headin' east, but that's the last anyone's heard of 'em. Personally, I think they took what ever they collected and headed back east. They wouldn't go south, because they know Connolly's people will be lookin' for 'em."

Griswalt overheard the conversation and took relief in the idea of this official thinking the two men simply absconded with the tax money.

"Let's take a look at that letter," Smith said. "I'm not sure it will do any good, but I'm all for sending it."

Smith and Mackay studied the document for some time before Mackay looked up and called to Griswalt, "Bring us a quill and ink please."

The two magistrates signed under St. Clair's signature and handed the paper back to him. "I'll get this posted with the first rider going east," St. Clair promised. "If Governor Penn can get the Privy Council to put pressure on Dunmore we may stand a chance of havin' peace around here. But if he's so land hungry as to take an army into the Ohio and Kentucky territories, I don't hold much hope of him listening to anyone."

Griswalt came up to the table and handed the men a sheet of paper. "Have you seen this?" he questioned. "I had it stuck on my door a week or so ago."

"Why, it says marshal law exists, and any act opposing the laws of Virginia will be treated as an act of war, and those causing such acts will be treated as a traitor and dealt with accordingly," St. Clair read. "It's signed by John Connolly, Captain Commandant of Fort Dunmore and Magistrate of Augusta County, Virginia."

"He has, in effect, declared war on Pennsylvania," Smith observed. "Is there room to put that in the letter?"

Laying their letter back on the table this bit of information was added.

"When I was at Williamsburg," Mackay said, "word was goin' around that a gang dressed like Indians raided the ships in Boston harbor. They were full of tea, and the ship owners hadn't paid the tax, and time had run out. The Crown was to confiscate the cargo and ships. Well, this gang came a whoopin' down, and damn if they didn't dump the tea in the harbor. That really caused a ruckus and there is talk of closing the port. The next thing ya know they'll be shootin' at the troops."

"That gang in Massachusetts are real hot heads," Smith agreed with a slight smile.

St. Clair spoke up, "You got to remember, they live a different life up there. The British troops are everywhere and I heard they was even tryin' to take the militia's canon and powder away from 'em."

Mackay added, "The idea of a Continental Congress was proposed by Mr. Benjamin Franklin, according to the delegation that came down from Pennsylvania when I was there. That didn't sit well with Lord Dunmore, but the colonial boys were receptive to the idea. With the mess in the Northeastern colonies, the Crown fears any alliance between the colonies would be the start of an independence movement."

"I can't believe Franklin had that in mind, "St. Clair disagreed, "He just wants the colonies to have more say in the governing of their affairs."

Smith broke in, "Franklin also is in a land deal with Washington, Henry, and others, I heard. They want to develop land in the Ohio Territory and even beyond. Maybe it would be to their best interest to help us clean up this mess Connolly has created."

"Maybe, but don't count on it," St. Clair stated sourly.

* * * *

"Margaret, you sure Jenny's strong enough to make the trip and live alone with Sam?" Amos Mock asked his wife.

"She's fine, and Sam'll take good care of her," Margaret replied. "Sam's bringin' up the wagon and team now."

Amos just shook his head and said, "I wish we could all stay together while these Virginians is still around. You heard they declared war on Pennsylvania, didn't ya? More tax collectors may be showin' up any day."

It had been over a decade since the Mocks had settled in the little valley. The years had been hard; even without the Indian raids it was a struggle to simply survive. They were fortunate in that they brought their belongings from the East in a wagon pulled by oxen. The beasts were strong and had saved many days of backbreaking labor, pulling stumps and clearing the land. Over the intervening time, besides the cabin and shed built the first year, they now had a barn and chicken coop. An addition had been added to the cabin, and a well dug. Two years ago they were able to purchase a wagon and a team of horses from a trader that was passing through. For life on the frontier, it was a comfortable living. Their youngest son, Jonahs, was staying with Hans Schmidt, learning the blacksmith trade. At 21 years of age, he had grown into a muscular young man, and swinging the hammer and pumping the bellows on the forge had toughened soft flesh into solid muscle.

"Mind the ruts and wash-outs," Roy called from the barn as Sam was bringing Jenny out to the wagon. "Get as much plowin' done as you can in the next couple a days. I'll be up to get the team then. We'll use the ox here, but they're so slow it'll take all summer to get the ground ready. If ya' need me, I'll stay a few days and finish up plowin' the south field."

Sam just smiled; he knew his older brother was joshing him that he couldn't get his work done and would need help. "You just come and get the team," he called back. "I'll have everything plowed and disked by the time you get there."

Jenny had healed physically, but mentally she was still in a withdrawn world. A dark fear gripped her as she and Sam headed back to their home.

Chapter 5
A Town Under Siege

"What ya got in the wagon?" A dirty, rough looking individual snarled at Van Gilder as he drove his team into Pittsburgh.

Without considering the consequences, Van Gilder spat the words back, "What's it to ya?" He started his team at a walk.

"I'll show ya what's it to me," shouted the man who seemed to be guarding the road into the town. "I'm a constable a Mr. Connolly's, and you ain't passin' without payin' your due."

Before Van Gilder could answer, or raise his whip, another guard leaped on the wagon from the other side and knocked the maker of liquid refreshments off the wagon seat and onto the ground. Falling hard onto the dirt road he landed right in front of the first constable. Van Gilder lay stunned when suddenly heavy boots began kicking him with a fury only a madman could muster.

"Now ya know who we are, Dutchman, an' you'll pay us what's due or I'll give ya more a the same," the first bully stated.

Van Gilder realized that they knew who he was, as the name "Dutchman" was what he had become known as in the town. Gasping for breath and bleeding from a cut on his face he struggled to his knees. "I've got to make my deliveries before I get any money," he managed to cough out the words between spitting blood and gasping for air. "I'll pay you when I come back through."

One bully looked at the other and decided that may be the best solution with one exception. "We'll take a jug for our trouble now, an' another when you come back, plus what you owe for both comin' and goin'.

"All right," Van Gilder stammered, glad to get on with his delivery without any more violence. "Let me get up in the wagon and get ya the jug."

Finding a jug of his cheapest corn liquor, he passed it down to the constables. His team pulled out as pain welled up in his head. His vision was a blur and everything seemed to be swimming around in circles. He was forced to continually spit out the blood that kept seeping into his mouth. His first stop was Hornsmacker's tavern, and Charlie Hornsmacker was a good friend. Although Van Gilder wasn't sure where he was or even how to handle the team, the horses had made this stop many times before and rolled to a halt in front of the tavern.

"What happened to you?" Charlie asked as the team stopped in front of his door. "Here, let me help you down; we got to get you cleaned up. Maggie," he called to his wife, "get Harold and help me bring the Dutchman inside."

Harold, their son, was in his late teens and had been moving barrels of ale when he heard the commotion outside. "Pa, what's happened? The Dutchman looks like he's been beat pretty bad," the boy observed.

Charlie was struggling to help Van Gilder off the wagon and into the tavern. "Take the team and wagon into the barn, unhitch the horses and put 'em in a stall, then cover the wagon with as much hay as we've got. I don't know what's goin' on, but I don't like the looks of it." Then, as an after thought, "He got beat so bad, I'm sure there'll be someone lookin' for him."

"Pa, we're near outta whiskey. Should I bring a barrel in outta the wagon?" The boy asked.

"Later boy; right now we got to attend to Van Gilder," Charlie replied.

Maggie had a bed ready in the back room and was getting warm water to clean the blood from the wounded man's face. "Look here," she said as they stripped off his shirt, "there's bruises all over his body."

"Someone has kicked him half to death," Charlie snapped, "I'll bet it was them bullies down at the road. They's been chargin' people to come in and out on the road like they owned it. The Dutchman's tough; with a bit a rest, he'll be right as rain in a couple a days. Get him cleaned up and I'll go help Harold with the team and wagon."

Out in the barn Harold was unhitching the team when his father came in. "Boy, don't say a word about what's happened here today. We can't cover the wagon; there ain't enough hay. Maybe tomorrow we'll try and find out who he was to deliver to and make the drops for him. Right now, let's get our barrel off and into the tavern. Maybe we ought to take two in; no tellin' when he'll be able to make another delivery."

It was evening and Van Gilder seemed to be resting comfortably. He was no longer spitting up blood, and his eyes were open from time to time. Walt Grimes, the mail rider, was in the tavern for supper and a tankard of liquid refreshment. Charlie motioned him aside.

"You headin' east tomorrow?" Hornsmacker whispered.

Grimes looked puzzled at the secrecy but answered in a lowered tone, "Yep, goin' to Ligonier."

Charlie nodded, "You'll be goin' past Griswalt's, and I need you to do a favor for a friend. The Dutchman's been beaten by Connolly's trash and he'll be laid up for a couple a days. Tell Griswalt to get word to Mrs. Van Gilder that we're taking care of him, and as soon as he can travel, he'll be home. But, be sure and tell her not to come to town; these men are mean and lookin' to beat up anyone from the hills, including women."

"I'll do it," Grimes replied, "and he isn't the first one to get way-laid by Connolly's men. I'm surprised they ain't been in here yet demanding taxes."

Charlie's face tightened and his eyes narrowed, "They been here and collected. It's either pay, or get burnt out, or worse yet, beat to death," he declared bitterly. "I hear St. Clair and the others been writin' to

Governor Penn tryin' to get some help, but so far nothin' come of it. We need a militia that'll drive this trash outta here. I don't care if they're Pennsylvania or Virginia; all I want is an honest shake, which we ain't getting' from Connolly. He's tryin' to stir up the Indians by killin' peaceable ones that come to trade and parlay, just so's he can kill 'em all and take their land. Once Logan and his bunch get back here there'll be hell to pay."

"I suppose ya' know Lord Dunmore is in town calling on all the men to join his army to go into the Ohio territory and push the Indians out," Grimes whispered to Charlie. "He's promising 100 acres of free land to all that join his army, and there's some good men joinin' up. They's goin' to march from Virginia to the big river, and cross over into the territory that the Crown said set as Indian land back in '63."

Charlie shook his head and muttered, "I don't know how the Privy Council let's him get away with it."

Grimes smiled, "He's a high, muckitty-muck lord, born to the aristocratic life and power. How do you think he got to be Governor of Virginia? Did ya' hear what the Boston gang did? When the Crown decided to confiscate the ships loaded with tea because they hadn't paid the tax on time, these hot heads took matters into their own hands.   They charged the boats and dumped the tea overboard. Dressed like Indians they was, but everyone knew who the leaders were."

Hornsmacker hadn't heard that news and it brought a wide smile to his face. "I wonder what Symonds and Campbell, here in town, think of that? They bein' our tea merchants and all," he ventured, "I'll bet they're gettin' real nervous."

It was obvious that the governing powers from England were not finding favor with the frontiersmen or the men of the Northeast colonies.

Although, he had never had trouble with them, as Connolly depended on his bringing mail and news from the East, Grimes left at sun up, before the road guards were out. Still, the guards were an unpredictable lot, so Grimes preferred not to take any chances.

It was late afternoon when he walked into Griswalt's. Looking around, he noticed that there was no one in the tavern, which pleased him, as he didn't want the news he brought to get into the wrong hands.   And at this time, no one was sure who was with or against Connolly and his men.

"Walt, I didn't expect you for another couple a days," Griswalt declared with a grin.

Grimes held up his hand indicating he wanted to talk privately. "No one's about is there?" he asked. "I got to give you some news that we don't need spread around."

Griswalt looked worried. He didn't need any more news that could bring disaster to his tavern and trading post. He still had nightmares about the tax collectors that disappeared from his place. "No we're alone," he replied. "What's up?"

Grimes related the problem and all that was happening in Pittsburgh. Griswalt was a Pennsylvania man and patriot; he had no love for the highhanded Virginians, so he agreed to pass the word on to Van Gilder's wife. "Jonahs Mock is coming in today to pick up supplies for Schmidt; I'll have him go back by Van Gilder's," Griswalt planned.

"Mind him to be sure and tell her to not go to town, less she'll end up just like her husband," Grimes emphasized.

The mail rider hadn't been out of sight for more than a few minutes when Jonahs pulled up to the store with Hans Schmidt's wagon.

"Jonahs, how's your brother and Jenny?" Griswalt asked as he greeted the young man.

Returning the smile, Jonahs said, "I just stopped by their place on the way in; they're doin' fine. Corn's up and the wheat is showin' green over knee high. Looks like it'll be a good year. I'm thinkin' that maybe I'll stop by Mother and Dad's on the way back. I haven't seen them in over a month."

"Let's get these boxes of iron loaded, the freight wagon dropped them off yesterday," Griswalt muttered. "How do you like the iron comin' from the furnace over by Ligonier."

Jonahs shook his head as he replied, "It ain't as good as the stuff we got from back East, but it's a lot cheaper and easier to get. We can work it without too much trouble. It makes good nails and that's what we got most orders for."

"I got a favor to ask," Griswalt grunted as he lifted one end of a box. "I need you to stop by Mrs. Van Gilder's and give her a message."

Explaining the situation, Griswalt wiped the sweat from his face and continued, "No need to try and make it to her place tonight; just go to your folks and start out again in the morning."

Jonahs headed the team and wagon down the road toward his parents' farm thinking about the circumstance in Pittsburgh, not knowing the trouble had spread into the very territory he was traveling. Sam hadn't mentioned the tax collectors and Jenny's rape, or the fate of the two responsible.

"Well if'n you ain't a sight for sore eyes," Roy shouted as the wagon rumbled to a stop in front of the cabin. "Look at you, all growed up and drivin' a team."

Jonahs just smiled at the statements his brother made, knowing he was happy to see him and replied, "Ya think ya could help me unhitch the team and help me in the house? I been settin' on this board seat for most a the day."

His mother was just setting the table and was delighted to set another place for her youngest son. It had been a few months since they had visited with the boy, and they had a lot to catch up on. Sam and Jenny's trouble was never brought up as the fewer that knew about it the better. Jonahs told them about Van Gilder being beat half to death and the roadblocks that had been set up.

"I'm tellin' ya, we got to get a militia together to protect what's ours," Roy stated. "It's gettin' worse by the day."

His father looked at his son and said, "Just hold on boy, if Connolly's bunch get wind a anyone tryin' to put a militia together they'll have 'em shot for treason. The judges are tryin' to get help from Governor Penn and the Privy Council but it'll take time."

"Time we ain't got," Roy replied. "The summer will be most half over in a few weeks, and we haven't had one word that help is on the way. And from what we hear, there's more trouble in the East, and that's where all the attention is goin'. There's goin' be more tax collectors knockin' on our door, you can bet on it."

Amos shot his son a stern look, which was warning enough to not mention the tax collector problem.

"Them tax collectors haven't been up to the forge yet, but Griswalt said they been nosing around his place," Jonahs remarked. "I don't mind payin' some tax, but that bunch sounds like they enjoy beatin' ya up more than gettin' your money. By the way, Sam's got a real nice crop a hay for ya. He an' Jenny were out cuttin' it when I stopped by. I think I'd rather work on the forge all day than swing a scythe or hay rake. That Jenny's a worker; she was out there raking a field as soon as it dried. Her garden is chocked full; she's got a green thumb sure enough."

Jonahs missed the looks passed around the table from mother to father to son.

"I'll put the sides on the wagon and gather up a load in the next day or so. Got to get it before it rains. We'll need all we can get for this winter," Roy added to carry the conversation away from the subjects of Sam and Jenny.

Jonahs opened the mysterious package he had brought in. "Here's a present I made for ya Roy. Just cut yourself a handle and ya can pitch hay all day long." With that he handed his brother a brand new pitchfork he had hammered out of raw iron.

"Why, that's real nice work," Amos said as he inspected the tool, obviously proud of his son's craftsmanship. "We can put it to use tomorrow."

"We found coal up by the creek. It ain't the best, but Hans showed me how to get it red hot, that takes the impurities out, then it makes a fire you can really forge with," Sam said, smiling that his father was pleased with his work.

* * * *

"I got to get back an' deliver the rest a my barrels," Van Gilder told Hornsmacker as he sat at the table, finishing breakfast.

It had taken two days before he could get out of bed and not faint, and another before he was steady on his feet, but he seemed ready to go now.

"Just hold on, we'll help ya make your deliveries. But your friends is still out on the road collectin' toll," Charlie told him. "Harold and I took a couple a your jugs and doctored them up a bit. Ya know that weed they call hemlock? The root looks like a parsnip and shouldn't be noticeable in the drink. Well, we ground up some a them roots and flavored the liquor with it. It probably won't kill 'em, but they'll be sick for a time. So when you go back home, them's the jugs ya give those rascals. Harold's getting the team hitched up, we owe ya' for two barrels."

Van Gilder looked at him in astonishment, "Ya saved my life; ya don't owe me nothin'. I owe you," he said.

Charlie shook his head, "What about we pay for one barrel and the other will be your rent?" Then he slapped his leg and laughed until his side hurt.

"The team's ready," Harold called in from the back door. "I'll ride along and help make the deliveries, if ya don't mind."

Van Gilder smiled and said, "Harold, I'd be happy to have you help me, but only if I can pay you." He held up his hand as Charlie started to object.

Knowing he wasn't going to win this argument, Charlie held his tongue and nodded to his son that it would be all right to take the pay. Harold's face lit up as this would be the first real money he'd ever earned. Living and working with his parents involved food, keep, and clothes, but no monetary compensation.

"Dutchman, you're late," Dave Proper shouted angrily as the wagon rolled to a stop in front of his tavern, The Blue Boar Inn.

Then he saw the bandages still wrapped around Van Gilder's head and watched as the Dutchman held onto the sides as he got down from the wagon.

"What the hell happened to you?" Proper asked.

"I've been laid up a spell," was all Van gilder answered. "Can ya help Harold unload the barrel ya ordered? I got a couple a busted ribs and can't lift so good."

The rest of the deliveries went pretty much with the same rhetoric. Harold would explain a little of what had happened as he unloaded the whiskey, and soon the whole town was buzzing with the news. By the time they returned to Hornsmacker's, it was early evening.

Maggie Hornsmacker met them at the door. With the authority in her voice that only a mother can have, she told Van Gilder, "You'll stay the night. You can start home in the morning."

You don't argue with a woman who has made up her mind, so the Dutchman just nodded and smiled his thanks. Besides, his ribs were hurting so bad he was grateful for the invitation.

"Harold, ya did a good job a helpin' me. In fact, ya did all the work, so here's your pay," Van gilder told the boy and handed him a double days wage.

The rest of the money he had collected was concealed under the boards in the wagon seat, all but a few quid he would use to pay the toll. Plus, of course, the two jugs of special whiskey.

The next day, by the time they'd had breakfast and said their good-bys it was mid morning. Van Gilder wanted to be sure the toll collectors were on duty before he passed their station. Unbeknown to the

Hornsmacker's, he had left some silver coins in the kitchen where Maggie would eventually find them. He knew they would never accept payment, but it made him feel better to at least try.

"Well Dutchman, ya bring us the toll ya owe?" The first guard snarled.

"Yes, and a couple a jugs besides," Van Gilder answered as he passed the jugs down and handed the money with them.

For these men it is never too early to drink, so they paid little attention to the money, which they grabbed, and opened the jugs and took huge swallows.

"It's passable," the first one said. "Now get on your way and remember ta pay next time."

Van Gilder just nodded and slapped the reins on the team's backs to get them moving as quickly as he could. *I would love to be here to see them tonight after finishin' them jugs*, he mused to himself. Every bump and jolt of the wagon sent a pain shooting across his ribs, but he was on his way home and he was grateful for that.

Stopping at Griswalt's, Van Gilder was greeted with more news.

"Look at this newspaper Walt Grimes just brought in," Griswalt practically shouted as he waved the paper in the air. "The Crown closed the Boston Harbor 'cause a that tea party them fellows did last year. That'll set them nor-east boys off fer sure. And look here, it has an article sayin' Ben Franklin's idea of a Continental Congress has been accepted by the colonies, and they's plannin' it for this September. Maybe they can get our territorial squabble straightened out."

Van Gilder, stern faced just muttered, "Don't count on it. Ya know Lord Dunmore is in Pittsburgh tryin' to raise troops for a war with the Injins to get their land across in the Ohio Territory. If he can get all that land for Virginia, and after bein' told to stay out a there by the Privy Council, what chance do ya think we have a stayin' part a Pennsylvania?"

"You're probably right, but if he would take Connolly and his bunch with him it would help ease things around here," Griswalt replied.

"Connolly ain't leavin'. He's got to protect his interests here. I heard while in town that he's partners with Dunmore in some sort a land deal. If the Crown won't do anything, maybe we should get our own militia like the nor-east boys have and protect ourselves, not only from Virginia, but from those across the ocean also." The Dutchman had lowered his voice even though they were alone.

Griswalt looked up in surprise and said, "Whoa, watch what you're a sayin'. If Connolly heard that he'd have ya shot for sure. But I don't disagree; we got to get the right man and the right time."

"Yeah, I know, but it takes them politicians back East forever to get things done. From what I'm hearin', the pot's a boilin' not only in the Northeast but in Williamsburg too."

With a wrinkled brow, Griswalt stared at the newspaper again, "They barely mention that Lord Dunmore is raisin' an army to head into the Ohio Territory. I guess old Ben Franklin is stirrin' things up, but he's a politician so ya don't know what his motives are. It don't say nothin' about it, but from what the rider says him, Washington, Henry and some others has formed a land company and plan on expandin' west and south. The Crown ain't happy about it and is clampin' down on the militia's powder and shot. That may be why Dunmore is a takin' the men from Virginia, and as many as he can get from here, to fight the Injins in Ohio. He already got a fort at Camp Charlotte where Chief Cornstalk is headquartered. The chief's a Shawnee, and if he hears about Connolly murdering them Shawnee chiefs last winter he's not going ta be real happy with the white man.

"And look here, it says the Privy Council last year gave all of western Virginia, plus the territory south and west of it to a bunch that included our old friend Benjamin Franklin, and Thomas Walpole, Samuel Wharton and some others. They're calling this new colony Vandalia. What do ya think Dunmore going to say about that?"

Van Gilder looked dumfounded and stammered, "Why that's two or three land companies claimin' the same territory. There'll be fightin' for sure over that. Well, I got ta get home; the Mrs. will be worryin'. If ya find out any more news you can tell me in a couple weeks; I'll have another load to deliver then."

With that he went out the door and climbed up on the wagon seat. He had his team headed for his home and still in the hills.

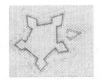

Chapter 6

A City In Chaos

"I'm tellin' ya, Charlie, the lid's gonna blow off this whole territory if somethin' ain't done. Those new guards at the road entrance ta here are worse than the last ones. I heard the last two took sick, and one threw up so much he busted somethin' inside and bled to death. The other one is still doctorin' for what ever it is they caught. Too bad the lot of 'em don't catch what them two got," Walt Grimes told Hornsmacker while he drained a mug of ale.

Charlie never changed expressions or made any attempt to reply. That hemlock root worked better than he ever imagined it would. *I can't wait to tell the Dutchman,* he thought.

"What do ya hear in Ligonier about the goin's on back East?" Charlie said changing the topic of conversation.

Walt liked to tell the news or gossip, either way he felt important to be able to hold the center of attention, and replied, "Well they's gonna have a Continental Congress this fall. I'm not sure where, but my guess it will be either in Philadelphia or Williamsburg. Ben Franklin been tryin' to get one for over a year, and they finally got all the colonies to agree. From what I hear, that Williamsburg bunch is pushin' for more say in running Virginia, and Franklin wants the same for Pennsylvania. Of course Dunmore's tryin' to squash the idea; he wants to run the whole show, Virginia, Pennsylvania and now the Ohio Territory plus Kentucky. Then ya got the boys in the Northeast shoutin' and carryin' on. Them hot-heads is gonna get more trouble than they bargained for."

"I can't blame 'em any," Charlie said. "They got the army breathin' down their neck, watchin' every move they make, and now with the port closed in Boston, a lot of 'em can't even make a livin'. From what I hear, the army wants to take the guns away from all citizens. If they's that worried there's more goin' on than we know about."

"Watch what ya say," Walt advised, "that fellow over in the corner frequents The Blue Boar and you know that's a Tory stronghold."

"Ya he's been hangin' around here the last couple weeks. In fact, it started just after the Dutchman got beat up," Charlie answered. "I suspect he's spyin' on everyone that don't cow-tow to the Connolly bunch."

"We got a lot a them Tories here in town, both from Virginia and here, but I'll bet there's more of us Pennsylvanian patriots countin' the hill folks," Walt muttered. "When push comes to shove how do ya figure we'll come out?"

"I think that even those that got their land from Virginia will go for liberty. If it comes to a showdown I wouldn't think Governor Penn would make 'em pay twice," Charlie's voice was almost a whisper. "Watch it he's comin' over."

Extending his hand the man said, "I'm Jordan Witherspoon, came up from Virginia and lookin' for a business opportunity."

Walt took his hand and asked, "What kind a business you in?"

"A little a this and that, anything I can make a profit at," Witherspoon answered. Directing his comment at Walt he continued, "You're the mail rider. I'll bet you know when and where there's money to be made."

"If'n I did I'd be makin' it," Walt replied with a smile. *No use getting him angry at me. Let him think I'm just a simple rider; maybe we can learn somethin'*, he thought.

Just then, over in the corner, a gruff voice shouted, "Tavern keeper, what do I have to do to get a drink around here?" It was Angus MacKerney

Angus wasn't the town drunk yet, but he was working on it. Charlie sighed and walked over to Angus' table. When he bent down to pick up the empty cup, Angus' hand shot up and grabbed his shirt and pulled him down, close to his mouth, reeking from strong drink.

"Watch what ya' say to that scoundrel," Angus whispered in Charlie's ear. "He's a spy for the Connolly bunch. I've seen him an' Proper at the Blue Boar cookin' up some kind a plot."

Then with a shove pushed Charlie away and shouted, "I can get a drink any place I want! If you won't serve me I'll go to the Blue Boar."

With those parting words Angus got up and left, cursing all the way. *It appears he's not the drunk everyone gives him credit to be,* Charlie thought. *What a great cover for a Pennsylvania patriot. Everyone talked freely in front of him believing he was so inebriated he didn't know what was going on.* Charlie walked back to Walt and Witherspoon muttering to himself, *Ya just don't know who your friends are.*

Witherspoon smiled a big toothy grin and said, "Had to throw the drunk out, did ya?"

Charlie nodded, "It happens all the time."

Walt excused himself saying, "I got some work to do. Nice to have met ya, Jordan." With that he was out the door and glad to be away from the spy. *I know them Virginia people are tryin' to find out who is against 'em and who is for 'em,* he thought as he swung up in the saddle and headed for the stable. *But why?*

He hadn't ridden more than a few yards when out of the shadows a form appeared, dressed in black and blocking Walt's path. It happened so suddenly his horse reared up, almost throwing Walt to the ground.

"Whoa," shouted the intruder, "where do ya stand?"

Startled, Walt replied, "I'm a loyal subject of King George, now get out a my way."

With that he spurred his horse and knocked the man sideways as they rode off at a gallop. *What's goin' on?* He wondered. *I guess I'd better start carryin' a pistol.*

Back at Hornsmacker's, Charlie was wishing this Jordan Witherspoon would go away. Charlie had more important things to do than listen and answer his questions.

"You realize that this is Virginia territory, don't ya," Witherspoon tossed the question at Charlie like he was challenging the tavern keeper's right to be here.

It was the last straw. Charlie's patience was at an end. His face turned grim and his eyes flashed, "I got every right to be here, just like you, maybe more than you. Don't come in here tellin' me my rights. Now get the hell out a my tavern afore I take the bung hammer to ya," Charlie snarled.

"Don't get your back up; I'm just here on a social visit, but I'll leave if that's what ya want," Witherspoon replied.

Maggie appeared from the kitchen, fixed her stern look of disgust on the man, and said calmly, "That's what we want."

That made it plain he wasn't welcome, but he had found what he came for. Charlie and Maggie were Pennsylvania patriots. He wasn't sure about Walt Grimes, however, and that bothered him as he made his way to the door.

* * * *

"Walt, you and I got to talk," Frances Wiggleworth greeted the mail rider with these words in a serious tone.

Walt Grimes was a little startled but replied, "Sure Wig, what about?"

Wiggleworth's General Store was one of the best stocked in Pittsburgh and also served as the post office. Everyone shortened the name to Wig's. The storekeeper was a jolly fellow, a bit over weight and balding. The rosy, puffy cheeks and mutton chop beard accentuated the roundness of his face. Could anyone suspect this unpretentious fellow of heading a clandestine group of men plotting independence?

Walt picked up the aroma of sharp cheese as he entered; it drifted through the room piquing his salivary glands, demanding a taste.

Wig saw Walt's nose twitch and recognized the look in his eyes. "Would ya like a bit a cheese?" he asked.

"I would indeed," was Walt's reply.

With that Wig picked up the cheese cutter, pulled off the cloth covering the large wheel of yellowish orange cheese, and cut off a generous slab.

"Bring it on back," Wig said indicating the doorway to the back room where the living quarters began.

As they entered, Wig's wife asked, "Would you like a spot of tea to go with the cheese?"

"Why, yes, that would be nice," Walt said, looking somewhat stunned at the offer. In all the time he had been delivering mail to the post office, this was the first time he had been invited to the living quarters, and the first time he had ever seen Wig's wife.

As way of introduction Wig just said, "This is my wife."

They waited until Mrs. Wiggleworth served the tea and then Wig waved his hand, which was the indication for her to leave. Mrs. Wiggleworth disappeared into another room leaving the two men alone.

"Walt, we been watchin' you an' I think I can trust you," Wig said. "I'm sure you have heard rumors there's a group of free thinkers that are fed up with the taxes and bein' ignored by the Crown. What I'm going tell you can't go beyond this room; it would mean certain death if word leaked out."

Walt's eyes grew large at the anticipation of hearing some real gossip. "You can trust me," he told Wig.

"What I need is a way to communicate with others that feel as I do," Wig explained. "You are the perfect choice. You come and go throughout the territory, and nobody questions your whereabouts 'cause it's your job.

"Angus tells me you walked out when that spy, Witherspoon, was questioning you all at Hornsmacker's. Make no mistake that man is out to crush any resistance to Connolly and Lord Dunmore."

Walt was shaken to hear that Angus was telling Wig anything. "You mean Angus is with the freedom movement?" he asked.

"You figured it out pretty quick," Wig answered. "Never let on he's anything but the town drunk. His life wouldn't be worth a pence if they ever found out. It was him that jumped out in front of you when you left the tavern the other night. Just wanted to see what you would do when startled that way. If you had been one

Connolly's boys you would have said so, figuring that was who was stopping you."

"Is Hornsmacker with you?" Walt asked.

Wig looked straight into Walt's eyes and replied, "No. Do you think he's ready?"

"From what he and I have talked about, I think he's more than ready. He not only hates Connolly, but he's gettin' fed up with the way the Crown ignores us but wants all the tax they can squeeze out," Walt said.

It was Wig's turn to look surprised, "Watch what you say; bein' against Connolly is one thing, but bein' against the Crown is something that'll get ya hung. Not that I ain't with him on that thinkin', just be careful who you talk to.

"I'm going to tell you a name. It's who you will deliver our messages to: Griswalt. I know you know him, and he's the one who recommended you for this job. He may want you to take messages to Ligonier, but that's something you and he will have to work out.

"With Dunmore in town tryin' to drum up volunteers for his army, we got to be more careful than ever now. I heard he was at the Blue Boar last night recruiting. With the promise of a land grant to those who joined up, he's getting some good men, both Pennsylvania and Virginia frontiersmen.

"In fact, I heard that a fellow that had been with the Rangers, ten years back, joined up. By the name of Thompson I believe. From what was reported there are more ex-rangers signed up from the hills south of here. They were before my time here, but from the stories I hear, they were a fearsome bunch."

"Griswalt has told me stories about them and the fight when the Injins burnt his tradin' post down. We could use them now," Walt mumbled as he sipped his tea then took a bite of cheese.

"Be careful, and put this letter in your boot. We can't afford to have it fall into the wrong hands," Wig said.

Walt got up and looked Wig straight in the eye, "Don't you worry; I'll be extra careful. Got any other mail to take to Ligonier?"

Wig shook his head, "No that's all for now, but I'll have more in the morning for you. Everyone knows that's the day you make the trip."

It was early evening when Walt arrived at Griswalt's. Hearing voices as he approached the door he thought, *I'll have to be extra careful not to say anything about politics.*

Griswalt greeted him as he came through the door, "Walt, I want you to meet one a the best Indian fighters in the whole territory. This here is Tommy Thompson; he's joinin' up with Dunmore's army. Back in the ole days Tommy and the Rangers saved our hides more than once."

"Well, I'm happy to meet ya," Walt stammered. "Griswalt, I'm going to take care of my horse, an' if ya don't mind, I'll bunk in the barn tonight."

Griswalt looked a little quizzical but replied, "No, help yourself. There's grain and hay in the barn, and a stall if ya want it. After ya get the horse cared for come in and have supper with us, Tommy here has got some real stories a where he's been."

Now, how am I going to pass this letter to him with this guy around? Walt thought. *It makes me nervous just havin' it in my boot.*

Walt took extra time rubbing his horse down and feeding him, but finally he couldn't procrastinate any longer and went in to supper.

"Come on in," Griswalt called. "We just started. Let me get ya a tankard a ale, an' here's a plate, fill it up.

Tommy has just started tellin' what happened after he and Smitty and Black Jack left for the hills south a here. What's it been, ten years or so I think?"

Tommy took a large gulp of ale and started, "Well, we had just struck out south, and were about a days march when we ran into a bunch that were left over from the Bushy Run fight. Jack saw 'em first and we took cover, not knowin' if they had seen us or not. There was about 12 of 'em, and as good as we were, we didn't want to get in a fight with the odds stacked against us. So we just laid low and kept an eye on 'em. They was still wearing war paint, but the fight was out of 'em, I told Smitty. Jack's cabin was about a half a day away an' we didn't know if it was still standin' or not. So we decided to wait 'em out and then go on our way.

"Wouldn't ya know, all a sudden one a those braves lifted his head and sniffed at the air, just like a hound dog. That cut it, they started shoutin' an' wavin' their war axes in the air, headed straight for us. I know I can smell an Injin, but I never knew they could smell us. Anyway, here they come; Smitty laid his pistol beside him, and, kneeling, took aim at the first one. Talk about a surprised look! When that rifle went off, the lead Injin stopped in mid stride and just collapsed. Jack had picked another one out and dropped him. The one I had a sight on ducked behind some trees before I could shoot, so I swung on another and dropped him.

"That seemed to confuse 'em. Turns out there were eleven of 'em, and now there was eight. The ugly one rallied the others and on they came. We didn't have time to reload, and they didn't shoot their muskets, which we was glad of. Smitty popped the first one to come on us with his pistol. Shot him clean through the chest. From where I was I could see the ball push out that Injin's back in a great splat a blood. That put him down, but not out. He got to his knees, so Jack leapt on him and finished it with his tomahawk. Smitty was the only one a us that had a pistol, so we drew our knives and axes an' went at it.

"I went after the one that ducked behind the tree an almost got scalped. When I reached the tree where I'd last seen him, he wasn't there. I heard a rustling behind me, an' out of pure reflex dropped to one knee. It was just in time; a tomahawk sailed past my topknot and stuck in the tree. That was my opening--twistin' around I was able to stick him with my long knife right in the belly. He let out a grunt as I ripped the blade upward until I hit his ribs. Just about then another brave came screamin' at me, an' I was still half kneelin' with a knife in one hand and hatchet in the other. All I could do was throw the tomahawk as hard as I could all twisted up like that. The Lord was with me that day; the axe blade caught him square in the face, splitin' his skull in half with a loud thump.

"I was up now and pulled the tomahawk from the brave's face, his arms was still flailin' an' his legs a twitchin'. The one I'd stuck was just sittin' on the ground holdin' his stomach. A quick whack with the tomahawk ended his misery. Smitty had one down, and Jack another, then things got real quiet. We could all feel it. Lookin' around there wasn't a sign of an Injin anywhere. The rest of 'em just disappeared into the woods, which I was mighty happy to see.

"We packed up what we needed or could use, muskets, knives, and jerky, then found why they didn't use the guns on us. They didn't have any powder. Hard to tell where they were headin' to get a supply, but most of 'em wouldn't need it now.

"We was carryin' a supply of jugs from Van Gilder, and fortunately none were busted. So we went on to the cabin and found nothing had bothered it. When winter set in we ran trap lines and hunted some; it was a peaceable winter."

Walt couldn't help himself, "How come you're signin' up with Dunmore?" he asked.

"Well, I don't know much about politics, and don't rightly care if I'm a Virginian or Pennsylvanian; as long as they leave me alone, I won't bother them. But, the main reason is the 100 acres a land he's promisin'. Even if I don't want to settle on it, I could sell it. So I guess you could say money is my reason."

Walt could understand the reasoning but thought, *I'd best be careful, those that aren't with you must be against you.*

Griswalt too was now hesitant in what he was saying. He still felt Tommy was a man he could trust but this was not the time to take chances.

"I hear the army is gathering down in the mountains in Virginia. You goin' down there?" Griswalt asked.

Tommy smiled, "Naw, Dunmore is takin' one army and General Lewis is gatherin' us mountain men and trappers for the second army. I plan on bein' with him, but I don't fancy hikin' through the mountains, so I figure I'll take a canoe or raft and float down the river an meet up with them where they's supposed to meet

Dunmore. I can get within 20 or 30 miles of the meetin' place and hike in from there."

The ale had been flowing rather freely and its effect was showing on the mountain man. The call of nature forced him to step outside. This gave Walt the opportunity to hand Griswalt the letter.

"I was getting worried that I couldn't pass this to ya," the mail rider exclaimed with a sigh of relief.

Griswalt said, "Ya did real good. I don't think Tommy would ever suspect anything, but it's best not to take the chance. I have another one for you to take to Ligonier. Mind ya don't have a run-in with any Injins. There's been some on the prowl after they heard about the massacre of the Shawnee chiefs and that mess with Logan's family. Can't say I blame 'em, but they don't care who they take their vengeance out on as long as it's a white man."

Walt shook his head and replied, "I don't plan on losin' my hair. I'm going to bed down now; I may be gone by the time you get up, so I'll see you on the return trip."

"I mighty glad to have ya with us," Griswalt said. "I only wish we had some men like Tommy on our side."

Walt spread his blanket out in the hay loft, pulled off his boots, shirt, and trousers and laid down. It was late July and not a breath of air was stirring.

"Y'all mind if'n I keep ya company in the loft?" Tommy shouted from the door.

"No, help yourself," was the reply, and Walt was out and snoring before the Scottish frontiersman got his shirt off.

Chapter 7

Hill Country Justice

Walt had to pass Hanna's Town on the way to Ligonier. Armed guards were still at the courthouse door; which was Hanna's tavern, but served as the courthouse for Westmoreland County, at least in Pennsylvania's eyes.

One of the guards waved him in and called, "The judge wants to see you, and he's got a letter for Connolly."

Not saying a word, Walt got off his horse, tied the reins to the hitching post, and entered the tavern.

"You wanted to see me judge,' he asked.

There was a little contempt in his voice, but it had come out before he realized it. *Easy, don't get on the wrong side of the law, especially carryin' this letter,* he thought to himself.

Judge Crawford was busy working on some papers and motioned Walt over to the table. There wasn't another person in the room; it was obvious court would not be in session in the near future.

"Be sure and stop here on your return trip; I'll have letters for you to deliver to Pittsburgh," the judge mumbled.

"I'll be sure and do that Judge," Walt replied cheerily, trying to make up for the nasty way he started the conversation. With that he turned and made a hasty retreat out the door. Pulling the reins free, he mounted and rode off at a gallop, ignoring the cursing of the guard because of the dust he stirred up.

It would be evening before he reached Ligonier and he wouldn't be stopping for lunch. Jerky and spring water would do until he reached the Fox and Hound, his favorite tavern. It wasn't that they had any better food, or their ale was smoother than anyone else's, no, it was the golden haired girl that was the bar maid there. As he rode along he visualized this buxom beauty and anticipated her greeting, which always sent his heart racing and brought a flush to his face.

What's that over in the bush? His mind snapped out of the thoughts of female companionship as a movement in the trees beyond the trail caught his eye. He had started carrying a pistol and it was now in his hand. Spurring the horse to a faster pace he strained his eyes, looking for signs of treachery on every side. Suddenly, an explosion of feathers burst from beside the trail. A hen turkey and her pullets, about the size of large chickens, took to the air with a great beating of wings, spooking the horse into rearing up, and almost throwing Walt to the ground. Holding the reins in one hand and a pistol in the other required all the horsemanship he could muster to stay in the saddle. But he hung on, and, after a short sprint, the horse was again calm and moving at a steady pace toward their destination.

Off to the left, up on the side hill, he could make out through the trees the abandoned cabin of the Kinsey's who had moved back East when the Indian trouble had started years ago. *That's strange,* he thought, *there's smoke comin' from the chimney. Well, I don't have time to investigate now, maybe on the way back.*

Crossing the Loyalhanna Creek, he took the trail that paralleled the water and led straight to Ligonier. Once on the trail, he noticed horseshoe marks leading up the path to St. Clair's cabin on the side of the mountain.

The judge must be havin' company, he thought. *No time to stop now, that golden haired gal will be waitin' for me.*

The stream was low this time of year with only a few pools holding enough water to support the fish population. *Maybe me an' her can take tomorrow afternoon off and come down an' do some fishin',* Walt mused.

The trail was carved out of the side of the mountain that sloped down to the water's edge in many places. Great rocks of limestone jutted out of the side hill. It wasn't unusual for large chunks of these protruding monsters to break off and come thundering down onto the trail or into the creek itself. Finally, the trail widened out and a lush valley spread between the steep rock forested hills. It was easy going from here on into town, and rider and horse spurred on at a gallop. Then, there it was, The Fox and Hound tavern. The inn stood just inside the entrance to the village.

Walt swung from the saddle and bolted in the door. At first he couldn't see her. Then as his eyes grew accustomed to the darken room, he could make out a form, as it materialized into a blond vision of loveliness, at least to this love struck mail rider's eyes.

"Where you been? You were due a day ago. You think I'm going to wait for you forever?" the young woman demanded.

"Helen, my love, I came as fast as me horse would run," Walt replied with a wide grin on his face.

With that Helen ran to him and threw her arms around his neck.

"Is that any way for a respectable woman to act?" Walt joked and returned the hug with enthusiasm. "Let me tend to my horse, and I'll be back in to seek your delights."

Dropping his dispatch case on the bar, he went back outside and led the horse into the barn behind the tavern. A rubdown, fresh hay, and a spot of grain for his mount, and he was back in the tavern, only to find three men seated around a table engaged in serious talk. *I guess there'll be no playin' with the bar maid while they're watchin',* he muttered to himself. The aroma of roasting pork filled his nostrils, and a whiff of blue smoke curled toward the ceiling from the clay pipes two of the men were puffing on.

"Walt," called one of the men, "come and sit with us."

It was Squire Horner, the unofficial mayor of Ligonier. Those with him smiled and offered a chair. The Squire motioned toward the others and said, "Walt, it's best you don't know any names, what ya don't know can't get you in any trouble. Did ya bring me anything from Griswalt? Yes, we got word ya may be with us."

Walt was increasingly uncomfortable. He was carrying a letter that could get him hung or shot, and these men seemed to know about it. Perspiration beaded up on his forehead and he stumbled for words.

"It's alright boy, we're with you," the Squire said. "These men are from Philadelphia and carry some disturbing news. Now, give me the letter."

Walt was in a quandary, if they were really part of the conspiracy he had to give them the letter, if they were spies for Connolly he could be arrested.

Suddenly, from behind came Helen's voice, "It's alright sweet thing, give them the letter." With that she put her arms around his neck from behind and pulled his head back into her ample bosoms.

"Helen, you with them?" Walt stammered.

"Just like you honey," she cooed. "We had word you was going to be bringing us news from Griswalt and we been waitin'."

Walt reached down into his boot and produced the letter, which he gave to the Squire.

"Come on Honey, we don't need to know what's in that paper, an' we got better things to do," Helen said as she led the dumfounded Walt upstairs.

"We'll be ready for supper when you come back," the Squire called after them. His two companions let out hearty laughes then put their heads together as they studied the paper before them.

The Squire spoke, "We have to get organized, but secretly. Pittsburgh has got as many loyal subjects to the Crown and Virginia as there are those of us that want freedom. Williamsburg's leaders are so tied up in their land deals that they don't care what's happening to the country. Until it hurts their pocketbooks they won't join us. The whole Northeast is on the verge of erupting, and if they do it too soon we won't be ready and Virginia won't be with us."

"Franklin thinks the Continental Congress this September will unite all the colonies and force the Crown to give us more say in governing ourselves," the older of the two strangers said.

The younger man added, "It could work the other way and force the Crown to put more restraints on us, higher taxes and a military law. We have to be ready for that and what action we take if it happens."

"Griswalt says, from what Wiggleworth reports, Pittsburgh is tied up tight. There's as many loyal to the British Crown as there are who wish independence. It's hard to tell how many would stand that ground if a real revolt would start," Squire Horner stated. "We've got to bide our time and recruit as many quietly and secretly as we can, so we'll be ready when the time comes.

"Ah, here comes the happy couple."

Helen was leading Walt down the stairs smiling and laughing. Walt looked a little worn out, but he did have a smile on his face.

"I'll fetch you some ale and dinner," Helen called as she disappeared in the kitchen.

Walt looked at the Squire and confided he had some news, "I was past the Kinsey cabin on the way here," he said, "and there was smoke comin' from the chimney. I didn't have time to stop, but thought you might know who's livin' there now."

The Squire wrinkled up his brow and leaning forward said, "Walt, there's been a gang robbing the people on the trail lately. We been tryin' to find 'em but they always seem to disappear. With the military gone, and Connolly declarin' he's the law, we just formed our own vigilante group. I'll have them together first thing in the morning an' you can lead us to this cabin. I got a feelin' that's where these highwaymen are holed up. That is, if ya can still get outta bed after Helen gets through with ya." Squire slapped his leg and laughed until tears came rolling down his cheeks. The other two joined in the laughter, which brought a blush to Walt's face.

"What's the joke?" Helen asked as she set plates in front of each. "Jacob could hear y'all the way back in the kitchen."

"Where is the old goat?" Squire asked. "I haven seen him since I came in. Is he back there cookin' up some home brew, or poisoning our supper?"

Helen looked at the Squire with her hands on her hips, "He's got a suckling pig on the spit just for you, and maybe I should tell him what you said an' he could poison it just a bit."

That brought more laughter from the whole table and managed to take the redness from Walt's face.

"Old Jacob's one of us," Squire explained to the others. "He doesn't mind a little teasin'."

Just then Jacob appeared in the doorway with a huge platter supporting a whole roast piglet. "We got boiled potatoes coming and some watercress salad," Jacob declared as he placed the platter on the table.

Squire looked up and smiled, "Jacob, these are friends from Philadelphia, an' you know Walt. That's the finest lookin' meal I've seen in many a year, thank you."

"Pleased to meet you and enjoy your meal," Jacob said.

Helen came in carrying a large bowl of potatoes. "Your watercress will be here in a minute," she sighed as she set the bowl down. "And I'll fill your tankards as soon as I get the salad."

As she turned to leave, she reached down and pinched Walt's cheek, "Don't eat too much, we got plenty to do tonight." Laughing, she skipped back to the kitchen.

Walt again turned bright red. Others had come in for the evening meal and Helen flirted with them all. It was good for business, and when they finished and paid their bills she was told to keep the change.

Morning came all too soon and Walt really didn't feel like getting up with the sun. Helen rolled him out of bed and declared she had to go down and start breakfast. It was a struggle but Walt got his clothes on and went out to the pump to draw some cold water to splash on his face. Feeling awake now, he went to the barn and fed and saddled his horse to be ready for the trip to Kinsey's cabin.

"Come in and have some tea and biscuits," Helen called. She had a large slab of ham fried with sliced potatoes to go with the tea waiting for him. "There Sweet Thing, that'll keep you goin' until lunch," she cooed.

Walt smiled and put his arm around her waist, "You thought anymore about what we talked about?" he asked.

"You eat your breakfast and we'll talk about it when you get back," she answered.

As Walt finished eating the sound of horses could be heard stopping at the front door.

The door opened and Squire Horner stepped in calling, "You ready, Walt?"

"I'm saddled and ready to go, Squire," Walt replied.

With that he kissed Helen and went out to the barn. Reaching in his saddlebag he brought out his pistol, checked to make sure it was primed, and stuck it in his belt. Then he swung into the saddle with the ease of a young man.

As he joined the others he counted 12 including the Squire. Some were dressed in standard frontier buckskin, others were in farm clothing, and a couple wore cloths that a merchant might wear. All were armed, he noticed, and each had a serious look about them.

"It will be about an hour's ride unless you want to push it," Walt told the Squire.

"No, we'll need the horses on the way back. No use in tiring them out now. Besides, I doubt if highway men move about much in the daylight," the leader answered.

Walt took the lead at a slow trot. They would slow down to a walk when they came to the gorge and had to follow the creek path. It was a pleasant day for a ride, but not for the business at hand. They rode single file through the gorge, and then crossed the creek to the path, which opened up and two could ride abreast.

Soon Walt held up his hand and told the Squire, "The cabin lies just up ahead and on that hillside. You might want to send some men up through the woods here and come in from this side. Then when we get to the trail that leads to the cabin half of us can take it and the rest circle around and come in from the other side."

Squire Horner nodded his approval and chose three men to head in through the woods. Then he explained the plan to the rest. Walt led the way, and when they reached the path to the cabin, four riders started their circle to come in from the other side. The rest waited to give the flanking parties time to get to their destinations. Waiting gave the flies, mosquitoes, and gnats a chance to find them. Swatting and cursing these biting insects the men fidgeted in their saddles until the Squire gave the word.

"Let's move out," the Squire said in low tones. "Walt, you stay behind. I don't want you gettin' in a scrap that ain't your concern."

"I'll come in last Squire, but I ain't stayin' out if there's a fight," Walt shot back.

No smoke was coming from the chimney. Walt reasoned it either meant they weren't up yet or they weren't home. He secretly hoped it was the latter. The horses and riders were on either side of the building and two men in buckskins dismounted, drew their pistols and walked to the door. Walt and the others also had their weapons out and cocked. Reaching the door, the two pushed it open with ease and quickly stepped inside.

"Up with your hands," was heard in a loud shout, then silence.

To those waiting outside it seemed like hours before three dirty disheveled men stumbled out into the sunlight, dressed only in their underwear and bare feet.

Squire dismounted and shoved his pistol against the first one's face. "You been robbing the folks around here?" he demanded.

Walt thought, *That's a dumb question;, why would he say yes?*

The others had gotten off of their horses and proceeded to tie the men's hands behind their backs. The three prisoners hadn't said a word and only glared at their captors. Then from inside the cabin came a call.

"Squire come an' take a look at this."

"Bring it out so I can see it," the Squire called back.

Out came the first frontiersman with an armload of silver plates, jewelry and pocket watches.

"Now, where do you suppose they found all that?" the Squire asked. "Speak up ya no good highwayman. Those plates are just like the ones the trader described that was taken from him only two nights ago."

There was still no answer from the captives. One was looking wild eyed as the men began tying nooses in the ropes from their saddles. "Ya' ain't gonna' hang us," he finally yelled. His voice was high and squeaky from his throat being choked with fear.

"Ya been robbin' folks for over a month. What did ya think would happen when ya got caught," the squire shouted back.

None of the other vigilantes said a word. They just went about the business of making the nooses and carrying out the loot found in the cabin.

"Wait," pleaded the wild-eyed one, "we get a fair trial. Ya got to give us a trial."

"All right," the Squire replied, "Court's in session; how do you plead?"

"We ain't guilty a nothin' that deserves hangin'," the robber cried.

"Then you admit to the robberies?" Squire Horner asked.

"Yes, we did the robberies, but didn't hurt nobody," was the reply.

"Well, this court finds you guilty and sentences the three of ya to hang. Put the ropes up boys," Squire called.

A convenient tree was nearby and three horses were brought up. The prisoners were put on the mounts and the nooses placed around their necks.

"Move your horses out," shouted the Squire.

With a smart smack the horses bolted forward and were reined in within a few feet. It was enough to pull out from under the bodies of the highwaymen. Walt had never seen a hanging, and his stomach churned with revulsion when he saw the grotesque looks on their faces, and their legs kicking in the air until death overtook their bodies.

The hangman's noose with the heavy long knot is designed to snap the neck as the prisoner drops suddenly. Unfortunately, these frontiersmen were not experienced hangmen and the necks weren't snapped. Strangulation ended the lives of the three highwaymen, a painful and slow death.

One of the buckskin clad men spoke to the Squire, "We should a put sacks over their heads. I thought the boy was about to lose his breakfast."

Squire Horner looked at Walt, "We don't enjoy this any more than you do, but it's got to be done or the robbing and murder will just keep getting worse. When those inclined to rob someone, or do harm to them, sees

111

what can happen when they're caught, it changes a lot of minds."

"Did ya hear what happened to the Dutchman," Walt asked. "He was beaten half to death by Connolly's men for no good reason at all."

The Squire's face showed the distaste he had for even the name Connolly and replied, "Yes, and they'll get their comeuppance, but we've got to bide our time."

It was a quiet ride back to the tavern. There was no joy in what they had done. But it was the only law they had on the frontier, at least on this portion of the frontier.

Walt was to return to Hanna's Town, however, he was shaken by the morning's experience and knew it would be dark by the time he got to Griswalt's, so he decided to spend another night here. Besides, he had important things to talk about with Helen.

"Y'all come in for lunch," Helen called to the men as they rode up. "Jacob baked some bread this morning and it's still warm, just waitin' for you to taste it."

No one had much of an appetite, but warm bread and fresh churned butter with wild strawberry jam temped every last one of them.

"Helen, we got to talk," Walt said as he entered the tavern.

"After everyone eats, Sweet Thing," she told him. "Maybe we can take some fresh bread and jam down by the creek later and talk there."

As anxious as he was to find out the answer to his question, this sounded like the best he could hope for. Rather than go in with the others, he took his horse back to the stable, removed the saddle, then brushed the animal for nearly an hour. Finally, he heard Helen's voice.

"Are you ready?" she called.

Walt was more than ready. He came out of the barn on the run, picked up the basket Helen had brought, and they headed for the water. There was a favorite spot where they had been before, under a large willow tree, secluded and private, away from prying eyes.

"Here, try this with that jam," Helen cooed and handed him a large slab of fresh bread with a generous topping of jam.

Walt was as nervous as a cat in a room full of rocking chairs. "Come on, tell me you'll say yes," he blurted out.

Helen looked at him with her big blue eyes and said, "Honey, I do love you, but I can't get married just yet."

"Why not?" Walt demanded.

"We have everything a married couple has now," she said. "If I was married I couldn't flirt with the men at the tavern, and that's how I make my money. The customers pay to flirt with me. They don't know it, but when they say, 'keep the change,' it goes in my pocket. Anyway, we don't need a piece of paper to love each other. Don't I treat you right when you come through?"

Walt was devastated. The bite of bread and jam caught in his throat. He couldn't even speak.

"Don't take on so," she cautioned. "We'll get married someday. In the mean time, we can still have a good time together. Let's go for a dip in the creek."

With that she unbuttoned her blouse, pulled off her skirt and kicked off her shoes. As she finished undressing she said, "Hurry up and get those clothes off; the water's cold and we can't stay in too long. When we get out I'll warm you up and take that frown off your face."

It was an invitation he couldn't refuse.

That evening at supper Squire Horner gave Walt a packet of letters. "Take these to Wiggleworth," he said. "They lay out the plans the men from Philadelphia brought. It looks like the Continental Congress is a sure thing and the Governors are mighty upset about it. I guess the Crown is also. Pass the word to Griswalt to just sit tight; our turn is coming.

"The boys in the Northeast are gettin' rammy. The army is clampin' down and tryin' to disband the militia. I hate to think what will happen if a shootin' war breaks out up there."

"Squire, there's some folks I think we should recruit. The Mock boys, Sam and Roy, and their dad, Amos. They have said how upset they are with the way things are goin', and I'd want them on my side in a fight," Walt almost whispered.

The Squire looked worried but said, "Ask Griswalt what he thinks. If it's alright with him tell Wiggleworth, he'll give the final word."

Walt was still dejected over being rejected, but maybe Helen was right he thought, *I guess we don't need that piece of paper, and marriage wouldn't change anything.* Another ale and he felt even better. Soon it was closing time.

"Come on Honey, help me clean up. Then we can get down to some serious love makin'," Helen cooed as she came over to his table.

The next morning Walt was up at day break. When he came downstairs Helen had breakfast ready and waiting. "How do you do it?" he asked. "You know when I'll be down before I do."

Helen just patted his cheek and smiled.

Soon he was retracing the steps he had taken the day before. Shivers ran down his back as he thought about how he had led the vigilantes to the robbers and what had happened. *It wasn't my doin'*, he said almost out loud. *They deserved what they got.* But he still felt his stomach turn when he rode past the path to the cabin. He couldn't look up the hill towards the hanging tree. Spurring his horse to a faster gate, he put as much distance as he could between himself and yesterday's scene.

Then he was at Hanna's tavern. The guard saw him and waved him in. Tying his horse to the rail, he never said a word to the guard, but walked into the room that served as the court. Magistrate Crawford was still at the table and looked up at the intrusion.

"Hello, Walt, thought maybe you forgot, you were due yesterday," Crawford said and waited for an answer.

"I got tied up in Ligonier, Judge," was all Walt replied.

Crawford smiled, "How is Helen?" he asked

Walt turned a little red in the face but just smiled back. *Does everyone in the territory know about us?* He wondered.

"Here, take these papers to Mr. Connolly in Pittsburgh," the Judge said shoving a large packet toward the mail rider.

"Yes sir," was all Walt could say before his hasty exit.

Loading the packet in his saddle bag, he stopped and thought, *Boy, don't get these packets mixed up, or you'll be in real trouble.* Nodding to the guard, he set off at a trot, anxious to put as much distance between Hanna's Town and himself as possible.

Three men were leaving Griswalt's as he rode up. Two were dirty looking with clothes that hadn't seen a washing in quite a while. The other was dressed neat and clean. Pulling up behind some trees he waited until they rode off. *No use invitin' prying eyes or questions,* he reasoned.

He was just tying his horse to the rail when Griswalt came to the door. "Ya know who was just here?" he asked shaking all over. "That was John Connolly his self and two a his cutthroats."

"What'd he want?" Walt questioned.

"He's still askin' about those two tax collectors that disappeared. I was the last to see 'em ya know."

Walt didn't know anything about the mysterious loss of the tax collectors so he just shrugged it off and said, "I got some mail for ya."

"Come inside where we can talk. I need a drink," the tavern owner replied.

Pouring two cups of Van Gilder's best, Griswalt was visibly shaken. "That man is pure mean," he continued. "It's been what, two or three months, and he's still tryin' to find the two? I told him they left here pretty well liquored up and rode off east. I hope they believed me."

Walt thought, *Why wouldn't they believe him? Well, that's no concern a mine.* " I got some mail from the Squire for ya, and wait 'till I tell ya about the hangin'," Walt reported.

"Hangin'? What hangin'?" Griswalt asked.

Walt went into detail about how he'd seen smoke at the cabin, and the Squire figured it was the highwaymen, and the vigilantes caught them and hung them.

Griswalt's face went ashen, "That Squire is gonna get us all hung. Ya know what would happen if Connelly ever got wind a this? Them ya hung was probably his men. That's the kind he's got workin' for him. Don't ya breathe a word a this to nobody."

Walt hadn't thought about the consequences of their actions, and he turned cold at the thought of being hung. "Don't worry, I won't say a word," Walt replied with a definite quaver in his voice.

"Stay over an' have supper with me," Griswalt invited.

"Glad to," Walt replied. "An' I want to ask you about recruiting the Mocks."

"They'd make good men," Griswalt mused. "I'd be for it, but ask Wiggleworth when ya get to town."

After stabling and feeding his horse Walt returned to the tavern and had a fine meal with his new best friend.

"Wig, I got mail for ya," Walt said as he entered the store. He had made sure the store was empty before stating his delivery. Even a casual observer could spell trouble if rumors were started.

"Bring it in the back," Wig told him. "Is it from Ligonier or Griswalt?"

"Both," Walt replied. "The Ligonier mail came through Griswalt and he added some more to it. I got some for Connolly too; does he pick his mail up here? I never had any for him before."

Wig raised his eyebrows before answering, "No, take it over to his headquarters. Maybe we should look at it first," he said as an afterthought.

"It's from Judge Crawford in Hanna's Town. I don't think we'd better open it," Walt nervously stammered.

"No, we ain't gonna open it; that'd get you shot. I just wondered if we could see anything through the wrapping," Wig laughed.

Walt took the packet out of his pouch and handed it to the storekeeper. "I want to get rid of it as soon as I can. I don't like havin' anything a Connolly's near me."

Wig looked the packet over and handed it back. "It's wrapped up and sealed so I can't make out what's in it. Just deliver it, and if you hear anything when you're there let me know."

Not even waiting for Wig to open his packet Walt was out the door and heading for Connolly's headquarters.

"I got mail for Mr. Connolly," he told the guard at the door.

"Well, take it on in," was the reply.

Walt had hoped the guard would take it and deliver it himself. Now he had to meet this villain face to face. Once inside he immediately saw the man dressed in clean clothes that he had seen leaving Griswalt's.

"Bring it over here," the gentleman said.

Walt started over when he saw there was another man, finely dressed, with two men in uniform on either side of him. *Now what?* Walt thought to himself.

"Come on, lad," Connolly said. "We won't bite you. I saw you at Griswalt's yesterday and wondered if you had anything for me. This is Lord Dunmore, and I believe you're Walt Grimes."

"Yes sir, I am," Walt replied. "Pleased to meet you your Lordship." Walt wasn't sure what he should do, so he bowed as he handed the packet to Connolly. Connolly was smiling and acted friendly and pleasant. He wasn't at all what Walt had expected. *Could this be the tyrant everyone is afraid of? How did he know I was at Griswalt's? He couldn't have seen me, could he?*

"If I have a reply where can I find you? Connolly asked.

"You can drop it off at Wig's store, or I usually eat at Hornsmacker's," Walt said without thinking. *Oh, I shouldn't have said that,* he thought. *If he associates me with them, and knows they're Pennsylvania patriots, we could all be in trouble.*

"What's the matter boy? You look like you've seen a ghost," Lord Dunmore said.

"Oh, no sir. It's just that I never met royalty before. I'm a little nervous, I guess," Walt lied.

That brought a laugh from both men as well as the soldiers guarding them.

"Alright Walt, I'll find you if I need you," Connolly said and waved his hand toward the door.

Walt whirled around and left the building in a rush. Now he needed a drink. Stopping by Wig's on the way to Hornsmacker's he relayed the information that Lord Dunmore was with Connolly and there may be a reply to Judge Crawford.

"Give me a jolt a Van Gilder's best," he said to Charlie as soon as he entered the tavern and then he slumped to a chair.

Charlie Hornsmacker could see something had unnerved the boy and brought a cup filled with the Dutchman's new rye whiskey.

"Charlie, I had to deliver mail to Connolly and Lord Dunmore was there. I let slip I ate here if they needed to get hold a me for a reply to the judge's letter. Oh, I hope it don't get us in trouble." Walt was shaking so badly it looked like he might spill his drink.

Charlie just smiled and said, "Boy, you did good. You think Connolly didn't know you ate here? Why that Witherspoon reported that fact as soon as he left here."

That bit of confidence calmed Walt down and he smiled that he had made the right answer after all.

"I'll finish my drink, then put my horse up, and I'll be back for supper," he said proud of himself now that he thought about it.

Chapter 8
Closing Out Summer

"Walt, ask Griswalt to talk to the Mock's," Wig said as the mail rider walked in the store to pick up the mail headed for the East.

Walt's face lit up at the suggestion. "I'll do that, Wig, and I'm sure they'll be receptive. They're pretty busy this time a year with the vegetables comin' on and the oats, wheat, and barley ready for harvesting, but they'll be in Griswalt's in the next couple of weeks. Did ya get a chance to talk to Hornsmacker?"

Wiggleworth looked Walt straight in the eye, "No, but if you think he's ready you can approach him. Be careful, Connolly's gang has been watching me pretty closely in the last few weeks, so I don't dare talk to anyone that's not connected with the business."

"They know I eat there all the time, so there shouldn't be any questions about me going in the tavern.

Connolly has been sending a letter a week to Judge Crawford, and the judge is sending a whole packet back to him. I'd sure like to know what's in them," Walt replied.

Wig frowned and whispered, "I think I know what's been goin' on. Every time you bring a packet back from Crawford someone gets arrested. I figure Connolly's askin' for warrants on individuals and Crawford is supplyin' them."

"They's no one in the Hanna's Town jail; where are they?" Walt questioned.

"Connolly's sending them all down to Augusta County in Virginia, some place near Staunton I hear," Wig replied. "With half our fightin' men in Dunmore's army and gathering in Virginia there's not much we can do about it now. But our time's comin', mark my words."

Walt was disturbed at the thought he was bringing arrest warrants back from Judge Crawford and asked Wig, "What can I do? If I don't deliver the packets they'll know I'm on your side, and if I do some good men will be sent to Virginia, and who knows what's goin' happen to them there?"

"Just keep deliverin' the mail. If they even got a smell a us bein' in cahoots both a us would be in a world a trouble," Wiggleworth replied. "Some will go to jail; we can only hope they survive until we can get them out."

"I'll get to Griswalt's tonight and give him the word to talk to the Mock's, but I can't talk to Charlie Hornsmacker until I get back in a couple a days. I plan on spending one night at least in Ligonier," Walt said, no longer blushing at the kidding he was taking about his relationship with Helen.

"That must be some gal I got to meet her someday," Wig replied smiling. "There's no hurry to talk to Charlie, we've put it off the better part of a month already."

"Soon as I put my horse up we got to talk," Walt told Griswalt when he entered the tavern.

Griswalt nodded his head indicating that would be all right. "We can talk over supper. I got some pigeons from Edwin Johnson this morning. We'll have pigeon and biscuits with gravy; how's that sound?"

Walt's mouth was watering already, "Didn't know the pigeons were migrating yet. They still catchin' 'em with nets?" he asked.

"I guess so," Griswalt answered. "He brought me a couple dozen. Figure you can handle three or four of 'em?"

"You bet," Walt replied. "I can't wait. You want me to pluck some for ya?"

"You get the birds ready and I'll mix up the biscuit dough and clean up some greens. We'll have a feast fer sure," the tavern keeper replied.

It was a meal to remember. Walt had come to expect a big supper when he came to Griswalt's. The old gentleman had no one to cook for unless he got company or customers in the tavern, and they were becoming fewer and fewer. He was delighted to have Walt stay for a meal whenever he came through, which was now at least once a week, sometimes twice, one coming and one going back.

This week however, Griswalt was getting more company than usual. Walt wasn't gone more than a few hours when a bearded stranger came through the door.

"Yes sir ,what can I do for ya?" Griswalt asked in as friendly a voice as he could muster.

The stranger replied, "Why, Mr. Griswalt, don't you know me?"

"The voice," Griswalt said, "I know that voice."

127

"I should say so," the bearded one said, mocking the tavern keeper. "We fought Injins together and most likely would a been scalped if the rangers hadn't been here."

"Jacob, you son-of-a-gun, how long's it been? With your face all covered up like that I couldn't recognize ya," Griswalt stammered.

It was Jacob Mock who had left for the Ohio Territory years before. "I just came from Sam's and wanted to say hello before I went on to mother's and dad's."

Griswalt was all smiles. "Well, I'm glad you did. What you been doin' all this time?"

"Well, I got me a farm on the prettiest piece of flat land you ever saw, and I married me the local chief's daughter. That's kept me out a trouble, until now, that is," Jacob said. "Logan's got the tribes all stirred up, so the chief sent me home 'till it blows over. I came through Pittsburgh and darn if I didn't get a job goin' out to Kentucky to warn the surveyors about the war parties headin' their way. I want to spend a couple a days with the folks before I head out."

Griswalt filled a tankard of ale and sat it upon the counter. "Have a swallow on me," he said. "How's Sam doin'? He was in last month tellin' me about their garden. Promised me a bushel a cucumbers in trade for enough cloth to make a shirt and dress for Jenny."

"Ya still tradin'? Well, they're ready along with everything else. Jenny and mother have put up four crocks of 'em to make pickles and already started dryin' corn and beans. This year they even put in some dill. They claim it'll give the pickles a different flavor. They's even been makin' something Hans Schmidt showed Jonahs. It's shredded cabbage, darnedest thing, you shred the heads a cabbage and put it in a crock with water, salt, and vinegar. Got to keep packin' it down. And it stinks! If it tastes as bad as it smells it won't be fit to eat. Jonahs claims he eats it at Hans' and it's real good, so we'll see. Anyway, it keeps over the winter and that's what they need. So you'll be gettin' your cuc'es and any time now."

"When do ya have to leave for Kentucky?" Griswalt asked.

Jacob shook his head. "They wanted me to get started now, but I'm goin' take a canoe down river so I can wait until the end of the month. That gives me two days to get my visitin' done. I would a liked to stay a while longer and help with the harvest. With the two farms they'll need all the help they can get."

Finishing his ale Jacob gathered up his belongings and said his good-bye. "Time to get a move on. Thanks for the ale," he said as he strode out the door.

By the time he reached his parents farm, Sam and Jenny had already arrived with the news that he was on the way. Roy and his father had been in the wheat field cutting the grain stocks, tying them together into sheaves, and stacking them in upright bundles. Next would come the threshing. That work was abandoned for the day as they wanted to greet brother and son, who had been away these many years.

What a grand reunion! Amos had a turkey plucked and tied on the spit, ready to put over the coals of the outside fire ring. Sam had brought a variety of greens from their garden, and Roy brought out a jug of Van Gilder's new rye liquor he had stored away in the barn. Mother didn't approve of strong drink, but this was a special occasion. Jacob told about his farm and the fact his parents would be grandparents in just a few months.

"Well now, that calls for a snort," Roy shouted, "I ain't never been an uncle before."

The men raised their cups and the ladies held up their herb tea.

"Here's to big brother! Who built his own place and started his family; may they be healthy and strong," Roy said as he took a sip of the clear liquid.

It was never mentioned that all were less than pleased the new born would be half Indian and Jacob could not tell from their expressions. In time all would accept the fact, and there was no question the baby would be loved as a true Mock.

"You must bring the baby and your wife to visit us as soon as they are able," Margaret said.

Jacob smiled and replied, "Maybe this winter, Mother. Roy, you and I could do some huntin' like we used to. I miss those days we spent together."

"Well, brother, we surely can, and I know just the place where the deer are as thick as fleas and fat as butter," Roy came back.

The rye liquor had loosened Roy's tongue and warmed his heart. The turkey had been roasting and was now a golden brown. Jenny and Margaret had the sliced cucumbers and fresh peas ready as Amos carved the large bird. This was all done outside at a table used for these special occasions.

"Tomorrow I'll help you in the field, and then the next day I got to be headin' for Kentucky," Jacob announced. "Already got half my wage for the trip and I'll get the other half when I get those fellows out alive."

Roy's eyes widened and sparkled, "That's a trip I'd like to make. Just like the old days, remember when we tracked them Injins with old Snead? Now that was excitement."

Jacob came back, "You remember how close we came to gettin' killed? That's more excitement than I want."

"Me too," his father chimed in.

Sam, always the statesman, changed the subject, "What kind a crops d'you grow out there in the wilderness?"

"Oh, just like you, corn, taters, squash. We don't have any cucumbers though. Maybe I could take some seeds back with me; I do miss them," Jacob said.

The rest of the day was spent reminiscing. The following day he was in the field with his father and brother cutting wheat, tying it with its own stems, and stacking the sheaves for threshing. The following day he was up and ready to leave as the sun sent streaks of red into the eastern sky.

It was just before noon when Jacob came to the road block and the guard collecting toll. Somehow he had missed this on his way in, and he was amazed that a tollgate had been established on a public road.

"Ya got to pay the toll ta get through," The guard told him.

Jacob looked at the one making the statement, then to the other standing off to the side. "What if I don't," he said rather cheerfully.

The guard laughed and sneered, "Then ya won't get through, or ya'll get the beatin' a your life."

The one standing to the side started towards him as the other one picked up a club he had at his side. Jacob's hand moved towards the tomahawk in his belt. He never raised his rifle, just placed his hand on the weapon in his belt. These guards had learned you don't test those dressed in buckskin. They all seemed an independent lot and were ready to fight at a cross word.

"Well, maybe ya can pay us on your way back," the one that had been off to the side said.

"Yeah, that's what we'll do," said the other and stood aside.

"Now, that's mighty nice a you boys," Jacob replied never taking his hand from the tomahawk. Skirting around them in order to keep both in view, Jacob went on his way into town and down to the river's wharf and the ferry that crosses to the south side of the Monongahela.

"I got a canoe waitin' on the other side; how much to take me across?" he asked

"One shilling," the ferry keeper called back.

Jacob looked astounded. "What? It was only a tuppence last time I went across," he lied.

"Well, it's a shilling now and two if ya got a horse," was the irritated reply.

"I ain't got a horse just what ya see. Here, take me across," and he handed the man the money.

"We'll go just as soon as we get another fare," the boatman said.

"We'll go now or I'll have your scalp for my belt," Jacob shouted advancing toward the flat bottom raft.

"Alright, alright, but mind ya, I work for John Connolly and he won't like it," was the reply.

"Is that supposed to scare me?" Jacob sneered as he drew his tomahawk.

"I'm just tellin' ya, he'll have your hide for this," the river man stammered.

"Well, tell him to come on down river and find me if he's a mind to. Now get me across," Jacob was getting upset with this bickering.

The raft hadn't more than touched the other shore when Jacob stepped off. Looking up and down the shore he finally spotted a canoe pulled up on shore among the trees.

That must be it, he thought to himself and carried his gear to the craft, proceeded to load it aboard and shove off. He was well out in the main current when he heard shouting from the shore. There was a fellow waving his arms and shouting something that Jacob couldn't make out. Or at least pretended he couldn't. Something to the effect that it was his canoe and Jacob was to bring it right back. Jacob waved a good-bye and began paddling with renewed vigor.

Jacob knew the river traveled north before it turned west and then south. He toyed with the idea of stopping when it headed west and going over to see his family. No, the chief had made it clear there would be no protection if Logan and his band caught him. Best he keep on and get to Kentucky.

He knew it would take well over a month to reach his finial destination. That would put him in early

October, a time of year he dearly loved, cool crisp nights, warm, but not hot days, and the trees would be showing their splendor in gold's, reds, and various shades in between. As he cruised down the water, otters would slide off the bank at his approach, ducks and herons would erupt from the back waters as he passed. Tempted though he was, he knew that the discharge of his rifle could bring visitors he wanted do without.

*   *   *   *   *

"We'll take the wheat down to the miller on the creek. He he only takes ten percent of the flour he gets from the grain," Amos said to Roy as they finished flailing the sheaves in the barn.

Roy looked up as he bagged the last of the raw wheat grains. "That'll be better than us tryin' to grind it like we been doin'. We wasted more than ten percent foolin' with it."

"The weather's been good to us; we got enough corn and beans dried for both us and Sam. I tried one a them pickles and they ain't half bad. They're not done yet, but they'll be right tasty come a cold December day. We'd better take three sacks a shelled corn to the miller's also or we'll be runnin' short a corn meal", Amos stated.

"Dad, if ya don't mind, when we get all these chores done I'd like to get Edwin and do a little huntin'. We all could use the meat, and if we get enough I could do some tradin' with Griswalt for powder and shot, maybe a bolt a cloth. You could use a new shirt," Roy made the statement looking sideways at his father.

Amos just smiled and nodded his approval.

"Griswalt called out a greeting as Roy walked in the door, "By golly, we was just talkin' about you! Ya know Walt Grimes, the mail rider. Come on in an' have a touch a ale."

Roy was a little suspicious. Why would they be talkin' about him? As usual there was no one else in the tavern-trading post so he figured it must be something private.

"That's kind a ya," Roy answered. "What ya been discussin' concernin' me?"

"Well, actually we been talkin' about your whole family," Walt said. "Y'all know how things is a goin' in the territory. Taxes on taxes, toll roads, citizens gettin' beat up and jailed; we got real problems."

Roy just looked straight in the mail rider's eyes never saying a word.

"Ya also know there's a movement toward independence, I'm sure," Griswalt said in his most serious tone.

"I'm part a that movement," Walt continued. "We ain't ready to do anything just yet, but we's needin' good men who feel as we do to get ready for what ever happens."

Roy looked from Walt to Griswalt then let his eyes scan the room for any movement that would betray an unwelcome listener.

Stalling for time to let what was said sink in, Roy answered, "I'm not sure I understand what ya are sayin'."

Griswalt smiled and said, "I think ya do boy; it's all over your face. We're formin' a silent militia and want you, your dad and Sam to join us."

This was treason and Roy knew it. If they were caught they could be hung or shot; either way they would be surely dead. Finally he replied, "I can't speak for dad or Sam, but I'm ready. If ya want I'll talk to both a them; I've a mind they'll be ready too."

"That's fine," Griswalt said with a big smile on his face. "Ya know what a big chance we took even mentioning this, so keep it between us and your folks. Now wet your whistle with this ale; it's one a the smoothest I brewed in a long time. Guess it's because I kept the mice from a fallin' in and drownin'. Sometimes I wouldn't find them till I drained the whole batch."

Roy's mind raced back trying to think of the last time he had a pint here that tasted a little strange.

"Here's to us and independence," Walt cried out, and lifted his mug high before draining it.

"What I come here for in the first place was to find out if ya wanted to trade powder and shot for some meat and hides? I figure Edwin and me can get enough for our families and trade you the rest," Roy said.

Griswalt slapped him on the back, "Sure boy, I can always make a trade for meat and hides."

"Well, I gotta get over to Hanna's Town. Judge Crawford will want to tell me to stop on the way back from Ligonier to pick up his mail then on to the Fox and Hound," Walt said as he sat his mug on the counter.

With a twinkle in his eye Grisalt shot the question, "How is Helen anyway?"

Walt was getting used to the question and made up a standard answer, "She ain't ready ta get married."

That usually stopped the questioning but this time a new comer was present who didn't know the story.

"Who's Helen?" asked Roy innocently.

"Just a friend," Walt answered, which brought laughter from Griswalt until tears ran down his cheeks.

"They's been keepin' company for some time now," Griswalt explained, and let it go at that.

Roy thought, *Maybe I should take a trip to Ligonier and stop at the Fox and Hound, there aren't too many young ladies in these parts.*

Dismissing that thought, he picked up his ale, took a huge drink, and commented, "You're right, this is the best you've made in a long while."

That pleased the tavern keeper and brought laughs all around. Walt was out the door and on his way. Roy couldn't stand it any longer.

"Tell me about this Helen and Walt," he asked.

"Oh, don't get any ideas. They been goin' together for years. He wants to get married and she's not ready. But from what I hear she really loves poor Walt; she's just not ready to settle down," Griswalt explained. "Now, you talk to your folks, be sure and tell 'em we ain't ready to do nothin' just yet, but we got to know who we can count on when push comes to shove. The way things are goin' in the Northeast it may come before we're ready."

Fall was coming on fast. The trees were already shedding their leaves and the spring cellars at the Mock's farms were full of crocks, in anticipation of the winter months just ahead. The spring cellar was just a cavern dug back in the hillside where the spring water ran all year long keeping the temperature at a consistent level, usually about 20 to 30 degrees above freezing.

Roy and Edwin spent these leisure times hunting in the forests they knew so well. Elk were becoming scarcer every year, but they managed to bring home deer and an occasional bear. Bear hides brought a premium as they were coveted by the wealthy back East. Griswalt was busy smoking both deer and bear meat as did the Mocks. This time of year it was a land of plenty. Everyone knew, however, that before spring brought warm weather the food supplies would be on strict ration.

"You should have seen Edwin," Roy was telling his mother and father one night after returning from a three day hunt with Edwin Johnson. "Wolves must a smelt the deer blood and they were circling the camp site. Old Edwin picked up a flamin' stick and his rifle and walked right out to where they was. When one snarled and came in close, Edwin just pointed his rifle and shot that critter right between the eyes. Well, that sent the rest a 'em off into the woods. I'll tell you, I didn't sleep much that night but he did. When I asked him how could he sleep, he just said he knew I was awake and there was no sense both us stayin' up. He's got more grit than I've ever seen."

"You say anything about the militia that's formin'?" his father asked.

Roy shook his head, "No, I thought I'd better wait. He's not pleased how things are goin', but I don't know if he's ready to commit to a militia. Thought I'd wait a while before bringin' up the subject."

Amos looked stern and said, "Sam and I talked it over; we are with the idea and if it came to protectin' our property we'd be there. But, if we joined up and it came to a full blown revolution we'd have to leave the farms and go off God knows where. So, yes we're with ya, but no we ain't signin' up just yet ."

"I'll tell Griswalt next time I get over there," Roy said.

Amos replied, "Never mind, I'll tell him myself. Got to go over there next week anyway."

"When I take the grain to the miller's why don't I go on over to Ligonier and see about those two heifers

Squire Horner has for sale? We could use a couple a milk cows," Roy suggested.

"That'd be alright," his father answered. "It's a long trip; ya might as well spend the night at the Fox & Hound." He said this with a straight face but the twinkle in his eye gave him away.

Now how did he know I had any motive but buyin' cows, Roy thought? *Well, cows first and checkin' out this Helen is next.*

Amos made his trip to Griswalts and told him of the decision he and Sam had made. He also conveyed Roy's acceptance and mentioned the fact his son was going to Ligonier to see about buying two heifers the Squire had for sale.

Griswalt just smiled, "Cows ain't the only thing he's checkin' out. Walt Grimes let it slip there was a fair haired lady at the Fox & Hound and Roy's eyes lit up like a bonfire."

"I know," Amos said, "but let him think we figure he's goin' to buy cows."

"Alright, but I don't think it'll do him any good. From what I hear that gal is so sweet on Walt she can't see straight. It's time he found himself a wife though, I'll give ya that."

Amos just nodded saying, "Dorothy and Becky have some friends back East but they want no parts a comin' out here. They call it the uncivilized part a the country, and Roy wouldn't be happy back there, so he'll have to make do with what we have to offer."

"Back to the militia," Griswalt changed the subject, "we can count on you and Sam to defend what's yours, is that right?"

Amos wasn't comfortable talking about what could be a revolt against the Crown but said, "Yes, just like in the old days. We protected what's ours and our neighbors. You really think the Northeast boys will start something?"

The tavern keeper shrugged his shoulders, "At this point who knows. After that tea party nothin' they do would surprise me. What concerns me is which way will Judge Crawford jump? I've always had a lot of respect for him, but his signin' warrants for the arrest a our citizens leaves a question in my mind."

"I know what ya mean," Amos said. "But he may have reasons we don't know about. I'd give him a chance to prove himself before I'd count him out."

Roy made his delivery to the miller then headed the team toward Ligonier. With the wagon he had to take the over land route which added considerable miles to the trip. *I hope that mail rider isn't there,* he mumbled to himself. It would indeed be an uncomfortable meeting if Walt was also at the tavern.

Roy's first sight of the blond creature, as he walked into the Fox & Hound, took his breath away. "Excuse me, miss," he choked out, "is there a place I can bed down my team? And do you know where I might find Squire Horner?" It had been almost dark when he reached the tavern. Stepping inside was intimidating enough, but to practically bump into a girl with all the charms he had hoped for was almost too much.

"Why sure, handsome," Helen replied, "you can put the horses up in the barn out back, and the Squire will be in for supper any time now."

This was all said with batting of her eyes and a flurry of her skirt. For a man just off the farm the gesturers were a sure sign of approval. Roy couldn't get the team in the barn, rubbed down, and fed fast enough. He just knew she was taken with him. Stopping at the pump long enough to splash water on his face and wash most of the dirt off, he went back in the tavern.

"Squire, this handsome young gentleman would like to see you," Helen called to the man seated in the corner.

Roy's blood pressure rose about 10 points just listening to her talk. The Squire waved Roy over to his table.

"What can I do for you, son?" he asked.

Roy was still watching Helen and had to clear his mind before he could speak. "I understand you may have a couple a heifers for sale." Though he was talking to the Squire, he was watching Helen.

"She is something to look at, ain't she?" Squire Horner said with a laugh in his voice. "But spoke for I understand. Yes, I do have some heifers for sale. Sit down and join me for supper and we can talk about it."

The Squire was telling him how sound these cows were and what good stock they came from, but Roy heard very few words, his mind was completely focused on Helen. Then the crashing blow: two more men came in for their evening meal and Helen called them handsome and honey and swirled her skirt just as she had for Roy. The young man couldn't believe it; she was flirting with everyone that came in.

"Boy, you listening to anything I say?" Squire Horner asked. "I told you she was taken and just good to look at, that's all you're goin' get."

Disappointed, he could now focus on business and maybe purchase a couple of young cows. The Squire gave him directions to his farm and they set a time. Helen was called over and Squire Horner asked if his new friend could get a room for the night. Unfortunately, the rooms were all taken, but he could sleep in the barn if he wanted.

"No, no," the Squire said. "He'll come home with me. We'll leave his team and wagon here and pick them up in the morning. Ya know who this fellow is? He's saved this territory form Injin attacks just 10 years back. Why, he's a hero."

Helen rolled her eyes and patted Roy on the shoulder, "If any Indians attack me I'll be sure and call you," she said.

That was the final blow. Roy knew he had no chance with this young lady. Just then Walt Grimes came through the door.

"Watch this," the Squire said nudging Roy under the table.

Helen flew across the room, threw her arms around Walt's neck, and proceeded to kiss him in front of everybody.

"What did I tell ya? Ya got no chance at all," the older man said to Roy.

"Well, it wasn't a wasted trip," Roy replied. "I got two cows for my trouble."

That brought a loud laugh and slapping his leg by the Squire.

The next morning Squire brought Roy to the tavern along with two heifers tied to the back of his buggy. They had concluded their business the night before and Roy was able to haggle the price down to what he thought was a fair offer. Evidently the Squire thought so too as he accepted it and they shook hands on the deal. Roy hitched up the team, tied the young cows to the back, said his goodbyes to the Squire, and started off down the road toward home.

"Squire, that Roy Mock is with us," Walt said in low tones as the wagon crept out of sight. "I just came from Griswlt's and he told me Roy was with us all the way, but his brother and dad would only help if it came to trouble right here at home."

Squire Horner whispered, "Wish I'd a known that. I'd have bought him another ale. Well, he got a good deal on them cows, so I guess were even."

Roy was at a slow pace. His two new animals were not at all happy to be tied to the wagon, and they baulked and pulled at the ropes holding them. Roy would curse at them, threaten them, and cajole them, but it was to no avail. It was going to be a very long trip back.

Not expecting any trouble Roy had his rifle stowed under the seat along with his tomahawk. The only weapon he had handy was his long knife tucked in his belt. Then, without warning, the horses shied to one side and started stomping and rearing. It was all Roy could do to keep them under control. Still jittery, but at least controllable, he got them off the road and held in place. Now the cows were bawling and bucking with enough force to either break the rope or their necks.

Jumping off the wagon he heard a buzzing sound that once you hear it you never forget it. *Rattlers,* Roy thought, *but where?* Evidently they had been sunning themselves on the path and were startled when the horses came along. Timber rattlers were not uncommon and Roy had encountered numbers of them. He still had a healthy respect for all snakes and stood stock still while searching the weeds and brush for the area making this repulsive noise. Almost jumping straight up there was one right at his feet where he had landed when he jumped from the wagon. *The other couldn't be far off,* he thought. Careful not to make any sudden moves, he drew his knife. Holding it by the tip of the blade, he threw it straight down and pinned the serpent to the dust in the wagon track. Twisting and writhing the snake struck at the knife's blade, which gave Roy the opportunity to move out of the way and get a long stick to pin the head to the ground, retrieve his knife and slice off that fanged appendage. The body still squirmed and twisted but the business end was out of the way. *Now, where's the other one,* Roy thought. The horses were still skittish and the cows were bawling louder than ever. He didn't hear any more buzzing, so back on the wagon and get the horses moving out of there was his only thought. As he prepared to climb on a voice came out of the thick brush.

"If'n you don't want that kin I have it?"

Roy immediately recognized the squeaky nasal twang. "Tom, you old son-of-a-gun! Ya scared me out of a year's growth."

It was Hermit Tom, who lived up on Chestnut Ridge in a cave he had fixed up for his home. Tom didn't mix with people much, but he and Roy had become friends when Roy hunted on the ridge and shared his game with the hermit.

"Them's mighty fine eatin' and I could make a meal out this one," Tom remarked pointing to the still squirming snake.

"Take 'em and welcome to 'em," Roy answered.

"The other one skedaddled into the brush. Say, ya wouldn't be interested in a couple a nice saddles and bridles, would ya?" Tom asked.

"Where'd you get saddles and bridles?" Roy questioned the old timer.

Tom was out of the brush now and picking up the snake. "Well, it was a month or so ago when I saw the buzzards circlin' about a mile from my cave. I didn't pay it no mind until I heard the wolves a howlin' an' decided I'd better take a look, maybe shoot me a wolf. Their fur is nice and warm in the winter. Anyway, I came up on two bodies or what was left of 'em, and about half mile further on I found two horses that had been kilt. Looked like Injins' done the horses in and the men was too far gone to see what caused their end. I would guess it was the same Injins. Funny though, I never heard or seen them crafty critters; I must be gettin' old. I was gonna take them to Griswalt when I bring in my furs next spring, but if you want 'em you can buy 'em now."

Roy was stammering for words, "I'll take 'em but ya got to hold 'em till I get up to your place this winter."

"That's right by me," Tom said and disappeared into the brush carrying his prize still twisting in his hand.

I guess it was good Tom found them bodies. He never talks to nobody, and better luck still that it was me he said anything to, Roy thought as the wagon rumbled along. At dusk he made camp, fed the heifers, and tried to get some sleep. The next day it was well past midnight when he came down the path to the farm. A stall had been prepared for the young cows and they were so tired they went in with no trouble. *I can tell Pa about the saddles in the morning,* Roy mumbled to himself as he put the horses up and headed for bed. It had been a long day.

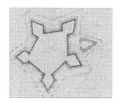

Chapter 9

Homeward Bound

"Ain't it a pretty time a year?" Thompson asked no one in particular as they followed the river bank north.

"It's even prettier since we still got our hair," Smitty replied.

"You best keep your eyes open; we could still be in trouble. This is Injin country ya know," Jack warned. "I don't trust these peace parlays, especially when made by the likes a Lord Dunmore and that renegade Cornstalk."

"Ah, he ain't so bad; he fights like he can never die and I respect that," Tommy broke into the conversation.

"You would," Smitty chimed in. "Sometimes I think they must a had Injins in Scotland and you be kin to 'em."

Tommy just shook his head, "Well, I figure they's just tryin' to hold on to their land. If'n I was bein' pushed out a my home, I'd be mad as hell too. I'm not sayin' I ain't doin' the pushin', and I was fightin' 'em to get 100 acres, I just see their point."

"You must be gettin' old ta' have thoughts like that," Smitty retorted. "I seen the way you kilt about a dozen or more a them defendin' their home."

"Well hell, they was tryin' ta kill me and you. I was just keepin' you from gettin' kilt. Ya don't find partners ya can trust every day," Thompson replied with a twinkle in his eye.

"When you two get through tellin' how wonderful ya are, maybe ya could pop one a them turkeys I seen scurryin' through the brush. I don't think the shot will bring us any visiters," Jack chimed in.

"Yeah, I seen 'em," Smitty replied. "I just didn't know if this old man could hurry fast enough to cut 'em off."

Tommy looked downright displeased. "I'll show ya who's an old man," he said as he took off after the birds. It wasn't long before his shot was heard, and a few minutes later he came back with a turkey slung over his shoulder.

Dropping the bird in front of Smitty he said, "I kilt it, you clean it."

Smitty never said a word, just smiled and began plucking the feathers. Once it was clean he took the carcass down to the river to wash it out.

"That was a quick wash," Jack commented as Smitty came hurrying back.

"It's clean enough," Smitty spit out. "We may have company. Some a Tommy's friends were here not more than a day a go. They's moccasin tracks all along the shore. 'Pears maybe a dozen or more."

"Maybe we should push on a bit further before makin' camp," Jack suggested.

"Suits me, how about you Smitty?" Tommy asked.

"I couldn't tell which way they was headin'; it looked like they might have canoes and just stopped for a short time. I would guess they's headin' down stream. Probably passed us when we cut inland back there a ways," Smitty ventured. "But I'm for puttin' some miles between us before we start cookin' this bird."

The sun had set before Jack asked, "Think this will do for a camp site?"

"Yeah, it's fine," Smitty answered.

Tommy just nodded his head in agreement and started gathering small twigs and dried weed stocks for the fire. "Wish we hadn't finished off that jug, I could use a jolt about now," he opined.

The other two smiled in agreement. The fire was small and the bird propped beside it. There was no time to let a proper bed of hot coals gather for roasting this fine supper.

"Look what I found," Smitty called as he came back from the river holding up a double handful of watercress. "This'll give ya a little pepper taste with the meat"

"I sure miss that jug," Jack commented.

"In a couple days we can pick up more of 'em," Thompson murmured. It was more of a wish than a statement.

After eating it was a fitful sleep for the three. They lay in their blankets with weapons primed and cocked. But the night went without incident and dawn came all too early.

They had camped where the river straightened out and upstream ran north by northeast. By cutting across country when the waters made loops they had saved considerable time and walking. About two hours into their trek Jack held up his hand. All fell silent. "Smell that?" Jack questioned, "Wood smoke. There is a trapper's cabin about a mile up river and I'll bet it's coming from there. I've poked around down here some and met him. Nice enough fellow, but there's too much smoke for it to be a camp fire. Best take it easy 'till we see what's what."

Quiet as any Indian the three maneuvered through the brush until they could see the cabin, or what was left of it.

"Burnt almost to the ground," Smitty observed, "probably late yesterday."

"I guess we was wrong about them canoes headin' down river," Thomson added.

"Just the same, take it easy. Tommy, you swing around to the left and, Smitty, you take the right, I'll go in straight. I don't fancy walkin' into a party of Injins on the war path," Jack stated.

In about half an hour the call came from Tommy, "Clear over here."

Then from the other side Smitty came into view and waved his arm showing it was clear on his side. Jack continued in and stopped to examine some tracks in the soft earth. "Looks like Tommy's friends were here. Ya see anything a the trapper?" he shouted.

"Over here," Tommy called. "Head's been split and his hair's missin'."

Jack and Smitty joined him and tried to reconstruct the action from the tracks. Foot prints and blood told the story of how the trapper came out of the cabin to greet the Indians, and then seeing they were not friendly, he made a dash for the woods, but too late. Bullet holes in his back then the mutilation of his body; it was all too common a sight from just ten years ago.

"I would guess Logan and some of his men are still prowlin' these parts," Jack told the others. "When we get to where the river turns north we can cut inland and up into the country where my cabin sits; if it's still standin'."

"Hard to tell where them heathens went, but I'm for that plan and get away from the river." Smitty replied.

"Me too," Tommy agreed. "Let's get this fellow buried and head out."

It was two days of hard walking before they reached the point Jack had described. Watching the trail and the river slowed their pace, but finally Jack declared, "This is the cut off. We go inland from here."

The further they went inland the more the forest became mature. The larger trees shaded out the brush and made traveling and seeing much easier. Vast stretches of oak and maple trees lay before them. The oaks had been dropping acorns, which squirrels were gathering and storing for the winter. Turkey and deer were also feeding heavily on these delicacies of the forest. Then the trio came upon a large area of chestnut trees. Again it was a banquet for wildlife. Hunting was the farthest thing from these frontiersmen's minds. If game was plentiful the marauding Indians would be close by stocking meat for the coming winter. It was no time to dilly-dally; all they could think of was to push on to Jack's cabin. Cold camps and jerky for breakfast, lunch, and dinner was their fare for nearly a week as they made their way through the great forest and steep mountains.

"The river's just over the next hill," Jack told his companions. "From there it's less than half a day's hike to the cabin."

"Can't be too soon for me," Tommy said stopping for a short rest. "We must a walked half way around the world."

Smitty smiled and said, "Ah, ya just gettin' old. Me, I never felt better."

Which everyone knew was a lie but the barb was felt by Tommy who just snorted and started walking again.

"Wait up ya cussed old fool! Ya don't have to prove nothin' to us," Smitty called after the departing old ranger.

Jack looked at the other two and shook his head. "Save your energy. We got a river ta cross and another mountain to climb before we get to the cabin."

The weather had been dry so they found a shallow point on the water and forded it with little difficulty.

"Now, just over that little hill and we'll be home," Jack declared as they emerged from the water.

"Little hill," the other two said in unison. "That thing's straight up."

"Let's take a break and dry off a bit before we tackle that 'little' hill," Smitty suggested.

"Now who's getting old," Tommy joked, but was more than willing to take the rest proposed.

"Alright ya old women, we'll take 15 minutes. I want ta get home," Jack told them.

They zigzagged up the steep hillside, trying to follow what game trails they could find. In some areas they had to go from tree to tree hanging on to keep from sliding back.

"Couldn't ya have found a steeper way up?" Smitty complained.

"I could have but you two old goats wouldn't be able to make it," Jack taunted back.

Finally, they topped the hill; below, in a little valley, Jack expected to find his cabin. "Would ya look at that," Jack said, his voice cracking with emotion. There was nothing but charred logs piled one on top of another, just the way they had fallen when the fire destroyed the roof and burned the walls.

"Well we can always build another," Smitty observed.

Tommy agreed, "There's plenty a trees. We can get it done in no time."

Jack knew they were trying to make him feel better but said, "Not with winter about to close in on us. There just wouldn't be enough time, and besides, we ain't got the tools we'd need.

"What say we rest up a couple a days and then head up to Fort Pitt. We could go over and see Griswalt, and VanGilder," Jack continued. "There should be some hides squirreled away in a little cave back yonder, so we ain't broke."

"Maybe we can hole up for the winter at Griswalt's. I'm sure he got enough chores ta keep us busy an' we can always hunt to bring in meat." Tommy added.

"Well, let's see if anything is left down there and set up camp. Too bad ya didn't squirrel away a jug while ya was at it," Smitty said with a rather dejected look.

Winter was closing in fast, so the first thing they did was build was a lean-to to break the wind and keep the rain and occasional snow off of them. It was a crude structure at best, but for the few days it would be used they felt it was satisfactory for their needs. The hides were found wrapped in oil cloth, and though the mice had gnawed away a few corners they were still salvageable for trade at Griswalt's. Otherwise found was an axe head, remnants of a shovel, and an old Dutch oven buried in the ashes where remains of the fireplace still stood.

Smitty had gone out into the forest early one morning and returned by noon carrying three plump gray squirrels. "Here's dinner," he called as he entered camp. "Didn't want ta mess up the meat so I just took their heads off," he said, bragging about his marksmanship.

"Ya wasted good powder and shot on scrawny critters like that?" Tommy jabbed. "Why, I could a kilt them with a stone."

"Well, ya don't have ta eat any, ya old coot. There'll be more for Jack an me," Smitty shot back at him.

Tommy just laughed and offered to clean the main course, as jerky was getting old to the taste buds by now.

Jack just caught the end of the conversation and said, "I'll gather a bunch a chestnuts that we can roast by the fire; my mouth's watering already."

On the third day they had rested enough and began their trek north toward Griswalt's. Their path wouldn't take them to the town where they had heard Connolly's men were challenging every visitor as well as the residents.

"Anybody know what month it is?" Jack asked.

"From the weather turnin' cold and the snow flyin' I'd say late November or early December," Tommy answered.

Smitty added his observations, "I'd say December."

"Well, what ever it is, the weather has turned nasty and we better make Griswalt's by tonight," Jack came back. "Even if we have to sleep in the barn it will be better than outdoors."

"Tommy, I guess we ain't the only ones gettin' old," Smitty said with a laugh.

"Here's where we ran into those Injins ten year ago," Jack commented, as they passed the area where they had encountered the war party. "It's gonna be late when we get to the tradin' post."

"Griswalt'll have something hot on the fire I'll bet," Tommy said. "I can almost smell it now."

"That's not Griswalt's ya smell, that's Smitty, and it don't smell like any stew," Jack ventured.

"Why, ya crusty old sod, ya don't smell like flowers yourself," Smitty came back.

"Alright, ya two old ladies, how far do ya reckon it is?" Tommy interrupted.

Jack thought for a moment then speculated, "At least two more hours, an' it will be plenty dark by then."

The night was clear giving enough moonlight to travel by, so it was well after dark when the three arrived at Griswalt's front door only to find it closed and bolted.

"Wake up, ya old horse thief, we need somethin' to eat," Tommy called.

Jack was banging on the door until finally a light appeared under it and a voice called out, "Who is it and what do ya want?"

"That'd be Griswalt," Tommy said. "It'd be Smitty, Jack and me.   Now open up!   It's cold as a mother-in-law's kiss out here."

With that the door swung open and the tavern keeper, framed in his candlelight, beamed a welcome to the visitors. "What in the world are you three doin' out, stompin' around on a night cold enough ta freeze the tail off a dog?" he asked.

"Why we came a callin' 'cause we thought ya might have a drop ta drink and a bit a stew fer our bellies," Jack answered.

"Come in, come in, I can fix ya up with a drop a Van Gilder's best and stir up some stew left over from supper. I don't get any visitors after dark nowadays," Griswalt told them.

The three stoked the fire and hovered around the heath as generous cups of whiskey were poured. As the stew heated they related the adventures of the past few months. Emphasizing their distrust and distaste for Lord Dunmore.

Griswalt looked at Tommy and said, "You were hell bent on joinin' that army. I probably should a told you what a scoundrel he and that whole Virginia bunch was, but didn't figure you would listen. Now ya know, and when I tell ya what's been goin' on y'all believe it."

"Well, I'm glad I went or I'd missed meetin' up with my partners here. Now, let me ask ya, can we winter here and work for our keep? Tommy asked.

That took Griswalt by surprise. Things with the militia were heating up at a rapid pace. *Are these three for the patriots? After what they said I can't believe they favor the crown, but maybe it is best to have them where I can watch and learn which side they're on.* "Why sure," he answered, "I'd be please ta have ya." Although it came in halting words, he hoped they didn't catch his hesitation.

A few days later Walt Grimes stopped in on his regular run and was surprised to see Tommy and be introduced to Jack and Smitty. The militia was starting to come together and he was especially cautious when he was around strangers.

After Walt had left Jack questioned Griswalt, "That boy acts like he's got something to hide; ya got any idea what it might be?"

Griswalt was in a bind. He knew if he lied Jack would read it on his face, but could he tell the truth? Were these frontiersmen ready to support a full blown rebellion?

Finally he said, "Yeah I do, but we can't talk about it now, maybe tonight at supper I'll fill ya in."

"All right," Jack replied, "The men an' I thought we might wander over to the Mocks ta say hello today."

That brought a grin to Griswalt's face. "They'd be pleased ta see ya, and why don't ya swing by Sam's farm and see what he and Jenny has done with the place?" he said.

"Good idea," Jack answered, "I'll gather up the boys and we'll start right off."

As was their custom, they carried their rifles and possible bags, more out of habit than necessity.

"Somethin's eatin' at old Griswalt," Jack told his companions as they walked along the trail. "I can't put my finger on it, but there's somethin' he ain't tellin' us."

"I noticed him and that mail rider was nervous as high bred fillies," Smitty answered. "They's both got something ta hide."

"Well, Griswalt said he would talk about it at supper, maybe we'll find out then," Jack speculated.

As they rounded a bend in the trail a rider appeared blocking their path. "You all been registered?" he asked.

"Registered for what?" Tommy responded as his thumb automatically cocked the hammer on his long rifle.

The action was not unnoticed by the stranger who changed his tone considerably, "Why, Mr. Connolly requires everyone passin' through or livin' in these parts to register so's they can pay the tax."

"I never heard a such a thing," Jack said and moved to one side as he cocked his weapon also. "Besides, we got no money; Injins wiped out everything we had an we ain't never got paid for fightin' down river."

"You fellows were in Lord Dunmore's army were ya? Well, I guess we can excuse the tax, but I need your names for the record," the rider explained.

Smitty was getting more agitated by the minuet and as he too cocked his rifle said, "Ya can get it from the army records. Now, if ya don't mind we'll be on our way, and if ya do mind we can settle things right here."

"Now look here, I'm a constable a the Augusta County Court an I'm out here to collect the names a everyone. I been authorized by the Crown and Magistrate

Connolly," the mounted rider said as he reached for his pistol.

"If'n I was you I wouldn't do that," Smitty observed, swinging the long barrel of his weapon toward the constable.

That was as much encouragement as this tax collector needed; he spurred his horse and took off back down the trail toward town.

"What a ya make a that? Tommy questioned. "We heard things were bad in these parts but tryin' to collect taxes for just walkin' on the road is too much. Maybe that's what got old Griswalt spooked; an' where the hell is Augusta County? Last I knew we was in Westmoreland County."

Jack just shook his head, "It don't make no never mind. Let's get on to the Mocks; maybe we kin be in time for lunch."

The three arrived at the Mock's just as they were sitting down to eat.

"Hey ya got enough for three hungry pilgrims," Jack called out as they approached the door.

"Well, I never!" Margaret exclaimed. "If'n y'all aren't a sight for these tired old eyes. Come in and I'll fix ya a plate."

Roy and Amos jumped up and with shouts and lots of backslapping to welcome the old rangers. Lots of stories were passed one to another: what the three had been doing over the last ten years, how they had joined Dunmore's army and been cheated out of the land promised, and the treaty made with Chief Cornstalk, The trapper's cabin they found burnt and his body mutilated, showing what this treaty meant to some of the Indians still seeking to drive the whites out of the territory.

"Logan's gang is raidin' all up and down the river," Amos said. "They don't abide by any treaty even if they was there to sign it."

Roy added, "I don't blame him much after what happened to his sister and family."

Smitty agreed, "We heard some drunken no-good slit her open and kilt the husband. I expect I'd be mighty upset if it happened to me."

"Ya heard about this John Connolly have ya?" Roy interjected. "He and his men been runnin' rough shod over the territory for most of a year now. The Crown doesn't seem to care one way or another; they just keep taxin' everything we buy. Some a us are gettin' fed up with the way things are goin'."

"We met one a them tax collectors on the way here," Jack said. "But we run 'em off tail 'tween his legs."

Amos looked terrified, "That's not good; he'll be back with an armed posse lookin' ta slap ya in jail. With the weather closin' in it may take a while, but you can bet they'll be a comin'."

"I guess we'll have to lie low for a while," Tommy speculated. "How many ya reckon they'll bring?"

"I would guess 20 or 30; they'll want the odds in their favor," Roy answered. "It'll be after the first a the year when we get the thaw, before real winter sets in."

Margaret, who had been quiet during the conversation spoke up, "Speaking a the first a the year, Christmas is just around the corner. How about you boys joinin' us for Christmas dinner?"

"Well, we kind a promised old Griswalt we'd have Christmas with him," Jack said.

Margaret wouldn't take no for an answer. "Bring him along. He needs to get out a that tavern for a spell. Roy here will get us a couple a turkeys and maybe a haunch a venison, and Sam an' Jenny will be here; we'll have a grand time."

"Only if we can help gather them turkeys and deer," Jack bargained.

"We'll make it a real hunt," Roy exclaimed excitedly. "I been itchin' to get back in the woods. Sam's got a couple a bee trees; he'll bring a supply a honey."

"Now that all sounds too good to resist," Smitty smiled. "I ain't had a Christmas dinner in I don't know how long."

"Probably before any a us was born," Tommy jabbed.

"We got a couple a horses and two cows since ya all was here last," Roy told them. "Want ta see 'em?"

"Sure," Tommy answered, "Ya still got them big oxen? I always admired them beasts."

"They's all out in the barn, come on out," Roy invited.

Amos said, "I'll stay here and help Mother, maybe we can have some pie when y'all get back. It was a good year for berries."

Once in the barn Roy became very serious. "Ya don't know what a hornet's nest ya stirred up runnin' off that tax collector. This Connolly has been throwin' people in jail down in Virginia for less than what ya all did. Maybe I'm talkin' outta turn but I think I kin trust ya.

Some a the people around here have been startin' a secret militia, to date nothin' organized. But if they come for ya, Griswalt can get word to the others and with a show a force and I'll bet they back down. If'n they don't we'll have our own battle. Ya heard about all the trouble they's havin' up in the Northeast. One a these days it's gonna come to shootin' and we need to be ready. I'd like to count on ya all when trouble comes."

Jack raised his eyebrows and said, "Ya can count on me for a scrap; how a 'bout you boys?"

"Ain't never backed away from a fight, an' if I can twist Dunmore's tail I'm in," Smitty replied.

Tommy was nodding his head in the affirmative. "I'm in; it's about time we had a say in what and who's governing us."

"Let's go in and get some a that pie," Roy smiled, "but don't say anything to Mother or Dad; the less they know about it the better."

Back at Griswalt's the trio explained what had happened on the trail and Roy's conversation. Griswalt looked more concerned than they had ever seen him.

"Boys, ya got ta keep this under your hat. We ain't ready for a shoot-out with that bunch, an' so far they got more guns than we have. On the bright side, I'd like ta have Christmas dinner with my friends. Sure beats us cookin' it ourselves."

Jack, looking thoughtful and scratching his beard, had an idea. "What if'n we round up as many a the old rangers as we kin find, and as many new ones as we can trust? We could have a pretty good force. And if it comes to shootin', there ain't many that could stand up ta us," he said.

"Right after Christmas we kin start spreadin' out to look for our fellows. I heard some went north so they shouldn't be too hard ta find," Smitty suggested.

"I'd like ta find old Snead," Tommy put in, "but he's probably dead and gone by now."

"No, I heard he's livin' with a squaw up Venango way. It might pay to make a trip up there ta see him," Griswalt answered.

"We'll do it," Jack said, "an' maybe he'll know some more that would like ta join us if the fight starts."

Griswalt broke in saying, "Not if, when, the fight starts."

Smitty, rubbing his hands together, exclaimed, "First we got a hunt comin' up and Christmas dinner, then we'll start out.

Christmas was over and the weather had brightened. Snow blanketed the countryside but the wind had died down and the sky was a bright blue. It was an unusually beautiful winter day.

"Time we got started," Jack told the others, "We'll be back in no more than 10 days," he said to Griswalt. "I'll head up to Venango, maybe Smitty can drop down where Frazier's cabin was, and Tommy, you want to check out the country up by Van Gilders?"

All nodded and picked up their packs and rifles while heading out the door.

"Tommy and me won't be more an a couple a days so we'll be back and then start out in another direction," Smitty told Griswalt as he went out the door.

* * * *

"Snead, ya old scalp taker, what ya been doin' these past 10 years?" Jack called out to the grizzled old man standing in the door of the remote cabin.

"Captain Black Jack, ya old son-of-a-sea-cook, I'd know that voice anywhere," came the reply. "How'd ya find me?"

Jack laughed, "I asked at some cabins where the old fort used to be, where the orneriest, most miserable man in these parts was and they sent me right to you," Jack replied.

"Come in, come in," Snead called. "It's too dang cold ta be standin' out here a jawin'."

The cabin wasn't much, one room with a fireplace which was blazing, furnishing just enough heat to make it livable inside. A plump Indian woman had brought the kettle from the fire and was preparing tea for them.

"This be my woman," Snead exclaimed, waving his hand toward the woman.

Jack explained his mission wondering if this old timer could still shoot a rifle.

"I knowed we'd come ta a shootin' war one a these days," Snead said. "Yes, I do know some that might make good rangers and I still got enough grit ta stand my part. We'll go out in the morning and visit these fellows. In the mean time, ya can stay with us. Ya want ta sleep with my woman?" He asked in a matter of fact way.

"No, but thanks anyway, Jack replied, "I'll be fine by the fire." Hoping he didn't insult either the host or hostess.

"Well, it's gettin' toward supper time and I got somethin' better than this dang tea," Snead said as he rummaged under the bed against the wall and came out with a jug.

After supper they reminisced about the Indian attack and Snead relived the ambush he and the others perpetrated on the Indian attackers of the Comstock family.

"Them were the good old days," Snead insisted as he poured another cup out of the jug.

Jack couldn't resist asking, "Where'd ya get the woman?"

The question didn't seem to bother Snead. "I bought her for five deer hides and half a dozen coon skins," he stated. "I was lookin' for someone ta cook and take care a the cabin, and ta keep me warm in the winter too," he laughed. "She does it all so it was a good trade."

The next morning the woman was up before either of the men. She had meat frying, tea made, and a hot porridge ready when they rolled out at daybreak.

Maybe this old coot ain't as crazy as he appears, Jack thought to himself.

When they returned that night hot stew was waiting and the warmth of the fireplace felt good as they had been out in the below freezing temperatures all day.

"Time for another snort from the jug," Snead declared.

Jack wasn't about to turn down that offer, and as they enjoyed the warmth of the liquid the talk turned to their visits of the day. All the cabins were out by themselves. These pioneers were a fiercely independent lot, and the thought of the Crown controlling their every move brought their blood to a boil.

Jack took a sip from his cup and said, "That fellow Snodgrass seems like he'd be a good one to have on your side in a fight."

"I wouldn't want to tangle with him, even in my younger days," Snead replied. "He and the rest a them are fed up with the taxes on everything we buy, an' if what you tell me about this Connolly happens here, there will be a revolution fer sure. An' we just saw five of 'em, I'll bet we could muster over a hundred if the time comes."

"Don't do anything 'till we send for ya," Jack cautioned, "If we tip our hand before we're ready the whole thing could blow-up in our faces."

Snead finished his cup and said, "We'll hold tight, ya can count on that. Now, let's have some a that stew the woman cooked up."

*   *   *

Walt Grimes came rushing through the door at Griswalt's, "I just got word from Angus MacKerney that there's a group a about 20 men gatherin' to come here and arrest ya three. Somehow they figured out ya been stayin' here and with this January thaw they's a comin' within the week."

Jack, Thompson and Smitty sprung into action.

"I'll stop by Mocks' place and get Roy ta come over and then head up ta Snead's and gather as many as we can get on short notice," Jack said. "Smitty, you go and see as many a your people as ya can, and Tommy, you do the same. We maybe got less than a week before they get here." Within the hour they were gone; their adrenalin pumping at the thought of being in a fight again. They may have claimed to be ready for retirement, but they thrive on action.

Two days later men began drifting into Griswalt's. These were mountain men, trappers, and farmers, all willing to put their lives on the line for the cause of freedom from tyranny. By the end of the third day fifty men had assembled. Snead had brought a fearsome bunch from the north, men who had fought

Indians and hacked out a living from the land. They asked no quarter and would give none.

Walt Grimes came riding in at full gallop, "They's a comin'," he told Griswalt and Jack. "About twenty of 'em, all armed and lookin' for blood. That's not all, I just heard that the court in Augusta County, at Staunton, was closed and they are movin' it to the fort in Pittsburgh."

Jack yelled to Snead, "How about you and your boys' stay here an' form a line in front a the building?" Then to Smitty, "String your fellows out along the side a the road, just outta sight, until I call. Tommy, you an' yours take the other side a the road doin' the same. Griswalt, you stay inside; I don't want ya gettin' shot. We wouldn't have no place ta stay," he reasoned with a smile. "Roy, ya stay with me. We'll face 'em down with Snead's bunch. Men," he called to the ones in front of the building, "if shootin' starts, scatter and take cover best ya can and pick your shots. If it comes ta that we take no prisoners; I don't want any a 'em gettin' back ta Connolly to bring more troops.

The men were in their places less than half an hour when hoof beats could be heard slogging through the muddy road.

"We come for the three that refused to pay the tax an' run our constable off," a rather unpleasant looking fellow said as he pulled his horse up in front of the group standing in the path. Long greasy hair hung down from his battered hat, and yellow teeth showed through his unruly black beard. Then he spat a stream of brown tobacco juice that landed right at Jack's feet.

"I wouldn't do that again," Jack said calmly, looking straight in the eyes of what he assumed was the leader, his thumb automatically cocking the hammer on his rifle. "I be one a them y'all are lookin' for. What d'ya want?"

"We come ta take ya ta jail, that's what," the big fellow called back. "See in how's there more a us than a you, I figure that shouldn't be too much a chore."

"That so," Jack replied, still with a calm and even voice. "All right boys, show yourselves," he called out.

Men emerged from the brush and snow, rifles aimed at the riders whose expressions turned from arrogance to astonishment. Most were clad in buckskin, some with bear skins draped over their shoulders. They made a frightful sight indeed.

"Now, there appears ta be more a us than a y'all," Jack said loudly. "Now ya still want ta try an arrest me?"

The leader's face went white, "Ya know we are the constables a John Connolly and Governor Dunmore. Ya're breakin' the law."

"Well, ya want ta try and take me or keep on livin'?" Jack asked. "If I was you I'd take my bunch back where ya came from and not even think about comin' back."

With that horse's were turned and started back down the road. The burley leader whirled his horse around without a word and followed his men. A cheer went up from the assembled men as the horses disappeared over the ridge.

"I've been thinkin'," Jack said to those gathered around, "they got a lot a our people locked up down in Staunton. If you fellows are lookin' for some action, we could go down there and bring 'em back."

Walt, who had been in the building with Griswalt, keeping out of sight, cautioned, "We'd better check with Wig first."

"You go and check with him; I'm startin' for Virginia and aim ta bring back the prisoners! How many are with me?" Jack called.

A roar went up from the men as jugs were passed around compliments of Griswalt.

Rescued

Chapter 10

"We'll leave at first light," Jack shouted. "What say Tommy and Smitty, want in on the action?"

"Ya know ya don't have to ask," Tommy said. "It's gonna be like old times."

"I'm with ya," Smitty chimed in.

"Snead you and your bunch and maybe ten or so others would make a powerful force," Jack said, looking old Snead straight in the eyes.

"Hell, we be for it," Snead replied. "I doubt if any a my guys would turn down an offer like this."

It was before daylight when these 25 hand-picked frontiersmen headed out into the darkness. They had to cross over the Laurel Ridge and by-pass Ligonier, to avoid attracting more attention than necessary. At this point in time no one knew who was siding with Virginia and who would send out an alarm. The thaw was over and winter had set back in. Cold wind whipped up snow swirls, limiting visibility and causing the men's breath to form delicate icicles on their whiskers. However, these men seemed to thrive on the discomforts and trudged on in high spirits. Once through the gap and into Maryland the climate tempered a bit. Soon Staunton lay just ahead.

"How ya gonna handle this?" Snead asked Jack.

"Well, I figured to just walk up, kick the door in, and take the men inside home with us." Jack answered.

"Sounds simple enough," Snead said. "Maybe a few a us should stay outside and cover any nosey critters that comes along."

"Good idea," Tommy spoke up, "I'll volunteer for that job."

"Me too," Smitty added, "might be the only action we see."

"All right, let's wait 'till morning. That way we'll have a day's march in before they can raise an alarm," Jack stated.

It was a cold camp, or almost cold. Small fires were made in sheltered coves to boil water for tea and warm their hands.

It was still dark when the twenty-five had surrounded the jail. Fifteen stayed outside covering all the windows in case some of the guards tried to escape.

"See if it's open," Jack told one of the men. "No use breakin' it down if we can just walk in. Well, look a that," he stammered, "they never locked it."

The ten rushed in quiet as feathers in the wind. The two guards were asleep on their cots, but they woke with a start when they felt the sharp point of a knife at their throat.

Jack held the knife at one and asked, "Where's the keys to the cells? Ya'll not be hurt if ya cooperate."

The terrified guard pointed to a peg on the wall where a large ring of keys hung. The other guard stared with eyes as large as saucers, trembling in his nightclothes.

"Tie and gag these two," Jack ordered. "A couple a you come back with me and we'll open the cells."

The prisoners had heard the shuffling of boots and whispered commands coming from the outer room. Not knowing if they were going to be moved to another jail or something worse they crowed back into the corners of the cells.

"We come ta set ya free," Jack told the men. "Make as little noise as possible; we don't want the whole town after us."

Smitty had come in as everything was quiet outside, "Ya got any winter clothes?" he asked.

One of the prisoners pointed to a couple of large trunks in the outer room and said, "They got our clothes and others in there."

Inside the chests were heavy coats, boots, blankets even hats of all descriptions.

"How many a ya are they?" Smitty asked.

"Six, no, seven," one of the prisoners replied. "There should be enough winter clothes for us all."

It was less than half an hour before the relief party and ex- prisoners were on their way back into the mountains.

"Connolly's sure gonna be peeved about this," one of the men speculated. "Might be if we have relatives away from the town we should stay with them for a while, 'cause he'll be checkin' our homes first thing."

Jack agreed, "That would be a good idea; we got him hopping' mad as it is. So if ya could lay low 'till we figure out what we can do it would keep ya out of another jail."

The hike slogging through the snow was a miserable experience, especially for those not hardened to mountain living. As the party started across Laurel Ridge a voice came out of the brush, "Roy, ya came ta get them saddles?"

"Tom, ya old son-of-a-gun, ya gonna get yaself kilt sneakin' around like that," Roy shouted.

"What saddles? What the hell is this crazy ole coot talkin' about?" Jack demanded.

Roy waved Hermit Tom in and related the story of where the saddles had come from and how Tom found them. Jack was a little more than impressed.

"My kind a man," he whispered. "Now, Tom, how much you want for them? We don't carry no money with us."

"Y'all look tuckered out. How about spendin' the night in my cave an' we'll work out a trade there?" Tom offered in his nasal, squeaky voice.

This was a first; Tom had never shown his cave to anyone before. Perhaps he was impressed by the size of the party, and the men who obviously weren't dressed for a march in the winter. Whatever the case, Roy and the rest accepted the offer readily.

After a roaring fire was built, and the men began drying out and warming up, Tom brought out a huge haunch of meat.

"Thought ya might like a taste a bear," he offered. "I already know what ya all been doin'. I went to Griswalt's a lookin' for Roy an' heard all about it. Got me a jug too; let's have a swig," Tom's statement was directed to no one in particular.

After passing the jug around, Tom spoke up again, "I figure ya don't want them saddles found, so if'n ya want I can make 'em disappear. I could use some powder and shot, if'n ya got any ta spare."

"I reckon we can do that," Roy said. "How much ya know about them saddles?"

"I don't want ta know any more than I already know," Tom answered. "An' that's too much already. I heard how ya stood off them that come ta get ya, and I was pleased we got some men with backbone around here. If'n ya get in any more scrapes call on me."

The men dried their clothes and warmed up over night before heading out toward their hiding places that would serve as home for the next few months.

Shots Fired

Chapter 11

The Blue Boar Inn was a beehive of activity, and the comings and goings of various residents were not unnoticed by Angus MacKerney, who reported them faithfully to Wiggleworth without any suspicion falling on either of them. The Tory spy, Jordan Witherspoon, was collecting as much information as he could on the town's residents. Unrest was at a fever pitch with citizens defying orders from Connolly's constables almost openly. After encountering the brazen hostility at Griswalt's the month before, the constables were not anxious to venture into the outlying countryside for fear the armed band may be hiding in ambush.

Concerned that a full revolt was immanent, Lord Dunmore sent word to Connolly to make amends with the Indians and secure their loyalty. Connolly, however, wasn't the person for this job after the atrocities he had inflicted on the Indians.

* * * *

Spring was slowly creeping into Western Pennsylvania, and rebelliousness was running high. John Connolly knew his hold over the town and its people was draining away. The only way to regain control was to defeat the gang of rebels hiding in the hills just east of town.

Angus MacKerney staggered into Wiggleworth's store and shoved a note across the counter. "Can ya fill this fer me; I'll be back later to pick it up."

Wig took the note and read, *Connolly's got all his constables gathered up to go to Griswalt's an' capture the rebels an' burn the tavern ta the ground. Appears there will be 50 of 'em.*

Just then Walt Grimes came in to collect the mail going to Ligonier. The store was empty so Wig spoke out, "Walt, get news to Griswalt—50 men are comin' to capture him and Jack and the rest. They plan to burn the store down and they probably won't be takin' many prisoners."

Walt turned and walked out of the store at a leisurely pace. He didn't want to cause any suspicion, but once on his horse he was off at a full gallop.

Spring rains had made the trail muddy but Walt kept pushing his mount as hard as he could. Once at Griswalt's he could rest and feed the animal.

"Ya got ta get outta here," he called as he ran through the door of the tavern.

Jack, Smitty, and Tommy were sitting down to supper with Griswalt and looked up startled. "What the matter boy?" Jack asked.

"Connolly's got 50 men ready ta come capture you and burn this place down," Walt spit out the words between gasps of breath. "I figure they'll be here by the end a the week."

"Best we start now ta get our troops," Jack said and moved away from the table.

Without a word Smitty and Thompson followed; each knew what he should do.

"I'll go on ta Ligonier and let the Squire know what's happenin'; he might want ta send some men ta help," Walt gasped. "After I rest a spell."

Griswalt said, "Walt, take my horse in the barn; yours is all done in. An' ya don't have ta stop at Hannas Town no more, the court's been moved, for the time bein' anyway."

The creeks were high with spring rains and the trails were muddy, but the three rangers made better time than most men could do in the daylight. Within two days the original 50 frontiersmen from the last encounter were at the tavern. As they were assembling horse hoofs in the mud could be heard, but coming from the wrong direction. The men scattered to take cover but then saw it was Walt riding beside Squire Horner. He had gathered another 10 men ready to fight.

Jack, out of instinct, took charge and spoke to those gathered, "Men, from what we hear, them that's comin' are out for blood, so this ain't gonna be a walk-in-the-park. I don't want us firin' the first shot; we got to look like we's defending ourselves. What I'm a sayin' is anyone that would like to head back home should do it now, an' no one will think any less a ya."

Not a man moved. It was Snead that spoke up saying, "Let's go down the trail a piece ta do the fightin'; it's no use a gettin' the tavern all shot up"

"Good idea," agreed Roy. "How about down at the curve in the trail where there's them big rocks we can use for cover on one side and thick trees on the other side?"

Jack smiled saying, "Sounds good. We can have most a us in the rocks and the rest about 50 yards up the trail. We don't want each side across from the other or we'll be shootin' each other. I'll be on the trail so's they'll stop, and when they take a shot at me y'all open up on them."

With the men in place, they were just in time before the mounted posse could be heard coming up the trail. As this was a wagon road there were three's and two's riding abreast, shouting and calling to each other, not trying to hide the fact they were on the march.

As the first horses rounded the bend Jack stepped out on the trail. "I hear you fellows are lookin' for me," he shouted.

"We come ta get ya alright," the lead constable replied. It was the same grizzled ruffian that had led the party in January.

"Come an' get me if ya can," Jack taunted as he cocked his flintlock and leaped to one side.

No one can be sure who shot, but a firearm was discharged from the mounted riders. The ball struck at Jack's feet, sending mud splattering up both his legs as he dove for cover behind a large maple tree on the side of the road. That shot sparked the beginning of the revolt in Western Pennsylvania. Although it was not against the British Crown, and these men were under orders from a Crown's official, no one considered it as a treasonable act, at least on the frontiersmen's side.

At the sound of the shot the riders on the far side of the bend spurred their horses forward just as the roar of black powder rifles and muskets echoed from the rocks above. Horses reared at the sudden explosion of noise. White plumes of acrid smoke blanketed the rocks from the discharge of so many weapons. Four riders fell from their mounts and were trampled beneath the hooves of the uncontrolled horses. Two others were bucked off, still clutching their rifles. The smoke was so thick neither side could see the other, but the posse fired blindly into the rocks. The whistling of lead balls ricocheting off the limestone blinds could be heard while those in ambush reloaded their weapons.

The riders were in total confusion; their weapons were spent and with the excited horses there was no chance of reloading. Suddenly, a light spring breeze swept gently across the hillside. As it whisked the smoke away in little swirls up into the trees, openings of visibility appeared giving the frontiersmen the chance that they needed. Picking their targets carefully, they fired, sending five more horsemen into the mud. Half of the remaining posse raced forward while the rest spurred their mounts to the rear and down the path where they had come.

Shooting could be heard from around the bend in the road. Jack dove for the shelter of a large rock at the side of the trail, as he sprung he pointed his rifle up at the leader and fired. The ball caught the rider just under the chin exploding up through his skull knocking him off his horse, leaving his men milling around, some trying to get a shot at Jack while others turned their horses up the trail.

"Don't let 'em get through, Squire," Jack yelled to the men stationed behind the trees.

As the horsemen reached the trees, a volley of rifle fire spat flames of death from the trees. Six mounted riders fell, two remained in their saddles until the horses bucked and threw them to the ground. The remaining riders whirled around and rode for the protection of the bend, not knowing that destruction awaited them there.

Abruptly, the two groups collided, those trying to get away by riding forward and those retreating from the ambush at the trees.

At last one of the posse took charge, shouting to his men, "Dismount and take cover." Half did as they were told, but the other half rode as hard as they could back down the road toward the safety of town.

"You cowards," he screamed after them, "I'll see you hung." His words held little weight as a 60-caliber ball struck him square in the forehead, dropping his body in its tracks, legs twitching in the mud. Seeing this, the men that had dismounted threw down their weapons and raised their arms. Surrender and whatever would happen after that would be better than dying for the small pay they received.

Seeing the upraised arms, Squire Horner and his men advanced down the trail, weapons at the ready. Jack called to his men still in the rocks to come down and round up the remaining force.

"Now that we got 'em, what are we gonna do with 'em?" the Squire asked.

Actually, Jack hadn't planned that far in advance. "Let's take 'em to Hanna's Town jail," he suggested.

That sounded good to everyone except Thompson who spoke up, "We ain't got enough food to take care a 'em. Maybe we should just kill 'em an' be done with it."

The captives, hearing this, turned ashen knowing this was a distinct possibility with these frontiersmen. One finally spoke with a shaky voice and near tears, "Listen, men, we was just doin' our duty an' got beat. If we promises to leave the country and never return would you let us go?"

Squire looked at Jack, and Jack looked at both Smitty and Tommy. "I don't know," he taunted, "kin we depend on your word?"

Smitty, with a very serious expression on his face, said, "Well, it would save us diggin' a bunch a graves and a lot a powder and shot. I think sendin' them back to Virginia might be best. I'd even let 'em keep their rifles since there might be Injins on the way."

"We won't come back ever," the prisoner yelled. "Would we, boys?"

There was a rumbling of, "No, we wouldn't ever come back," from the captives.

Squire Horner said, "I don't know, we could just scalp 'em and claim the Injins did it."

The prisoners were huddled together shaking with fear. "Honest, we won't be back. We're through with Connolly; ya can count on that," the one that had spoken up first said in a quivering voice.

"Well, alright then," Jack told them. "Bury your dead over there in the woods, take your weapons, but leave the rest here. A couple a ya round up your horses. ya might as well ride south."

"Yes sir, we'll get right to it," the new leader of the posse replied.

The weapons that had been dropped in the mud were useless until cleaned, so the victors had no fear that these men would try to retaliate with a sneak attack. Jack, Squire, Smitty, and Tommy could hardly hold in the laughter as their antics about killing these men was just to put fear into the captives. They had planned on releasing them all along.

Back at Griswalt's the men were in high spirits at having defeated the force sent out to capture them. Griswalt called Jack and the others over to a table in the corner, "Walt brought this newspaper in with him. Listen here to what Ben Franklin wrote: 'At the Third Assembly Convention of Virginia, held in Richmond last month, Patrick Henry made a speech saying, 'Give me liberty or give me death.' This is after Lord Dunmore attempted to remove the powder and arms from the powder magazine at Williamsburg. Patrick Henry, a Colonel in the Virginia Militia, called up his troops and forced Dunmore to return the powder and arms. It was then discovered that many parts had been taken from the muskets, which enraged the citizens of Virginia. The atmosphere in eastern Virginia became so ugly Lord Dunmore took his family and moved to a British war ship anchored in the James River. For his rebellious act Patrick Henry was branded Public Enemy Number 1 by the British government.

'Dunmore further alienated the Virginia population by building a marine force and raiding the plantations. He offered the slaves and indentured servants their freedom if they would join his army to quell this rebellion.

'Although the Virginia Assembly had pledged allegiance to the British Crown, they were now without a British governor and the Crown issued orders that all 13 colonies were in revolt.'

"Well, since we are in revolt I guess what you did to Connolly's men could be considered part of the revolt. Walt, you best get this paper in to Wig. We got to get our troops organized."

John Connolly's power was fast eroding, and he could get no help from Lord Dunmore who was having enough trouble of his own in Virginia. The fight near Griswalt's had taken its toll on the so-called constables and many had deserted to the south. Surprising to Griswalt and the Rangers, there had been no reprisal for the ambush they perpetrated on Connolly's men. The Virginia militia openly fought Dunmore's army, which consisted of not only regular British troops but also slaves he had recruited by promising them freedom. As Connolly's power shrunk the patriot forces grew. Wiggleworth's store and Hornsmacker's tavern became focal points for the patriots. As their forces enlarged, the Tories became increasingly worried; fear of retaliation from over zealous patriots was something they lived with day and night. It was no secret who was loyal to the Crown and who was in rebellion. Captain Jack was again organizing the Rangers into a guerrilla type fighting group. They were preparing for war.

It was early May when Walt Grimes brought the news of war. "I tell ya, Griswalt, this means a revolution fer sure. Look here at the headline in this paper I just brought: 'British Troops Fired On.' Them Northeast farmers done set it off. Says they got shot at by the

British troops when the troops was marchin' up to some place called Lexington. The militia of Massachusetts must a stood their ground and somebody shot, paper don't say which side, but that set it off. It don't say why the British was marchin' on the town either. But with that shot all hell broke loose. It says the British tried to retreat, but the patriots kept takin' pot shots at 'em and the longer it went on the more militia showed up. Even when a regiment of British regulars showed up the militia outnumbered them. Any way, they drove the British back to Boston. Men kilt on both sides, it says. We're in it fer sure now."

"We ain't ready for this yet," Griswalt said. "Don't let our boys get too rammy. Tell Wig we got ta keep a lid on this 'till we're stronger."

"Ya know we got that meetin' comin' up where all the militia leaders are comin' ta talk about joinin' the revolution," Walt replied. "It's only a couple a days away. This'll put some spark into the talks."

"Well the convention called the militia the Committee of Safety and approved the action of the other colonies in their revolt against the Crown. We'll have ta watch the Tories. We know who they are now; if they stay in town they could be spies for the British forces," Wig told Hornsmacker and MacKerney.

"I for one am glad it's out in the open; I'm tired a playin' the town drunk," MacKerney stated.

Wigelworth smiled and said, "Things must be gettin' too hot for John Connolly. I hear he's packin' up and headin' back to be with Dunmore. I'll be glad ta see the back a him, I'll tell ya."

"Ya think they'll give up the claim on our land?" Hornsmacker asked.

"My guess is the Virginia Assembly is busy enough without worryin' about who owns this part a the territory," Wig answered.

July melted into August, Connolly and his men had left for Virginia, his grand plan to own not only the land around the Three Rivers but the Ohio Territory as well had been exposed. He was now a fugitive from patriot justice.

The Committee of Safety was meeting when word came that a hundred Virginia militia troops had arrived and taken over the fort. Their leader, John Neville, sent word he wanted to talk with the patriot's leaders.

Walt Grimes was sent to bring Griswalt and Jack, while Wig and Hornsmacker prepared for the worst. It was two days later when the group from Pittsburgh went to the fort.

"I don't know what to expect," Wig said to his companions. "Neville own a powerful lot a land around here. I would have thought he'd be with us not against us."

"We'll soon know," Jack commented as they reached the outer gate to the fort.

Neville met them and ushered the group in to his quarters. "Men," he said, "I've been sent here by the Virginia Assembly. Not to harass you, but only to secure the fort for us patriots. This land claim has been going on long enough and the Mason Dixon survey has been completed. Dunmore wouldn't abide by it but the new Colonial Assembly of Virginia will. There's still some things to be worked out but they can wait until we get this revolution won."

Smiles broke out on each of the patriots' faces and Wig stuck out his hand saying, "By golly, Captain, ya got a deal."

On the way back to town they noticed smoke coming from one of the stores. "It's Symonds and Campbell's, the tea merchants," Hornsmacker called.

"I was afraid the boys would get carried away," Wig said. "We got ta calm 'em down or we'll be no better than Connolly."

"Spread the word that we're gonna work with Neville and his men. The Tories can stay or leave; it's up to them. Unless we find them spyin' we'll not bother 'em," Jack shouted as he ran toward the fire.

Roy, Snead, and his mountain men joined the militia ready to fight for a new country and freedom from the yoke of British rule. Men from every colony were joining their militia's ready to lay their lives on the line. They would be called on soon enough to join Washington's rag-tag army that would prove to be more than a match for the British and Hessian troops.

In November of 1775, John Connolly was arrested in Maryland and served the remaining years of the war in jail. After the war he was released and he moved to Canada where he lived out his life.

The heroics of the Western Pennsylvania fighting men are well documented in the historical writings of the Revolutionary War. We have to assume Jack, Tommy, Smitty, Snead, and the other frontiersmen were part of this fighting force.

END